MANGA MATH MYSTERIES

#2

THE HUNDRED-DOLLAR ROBBER

A Mystery with Money

by Melinda Thielbar

illustrated by Tintin Pantoja

GRAPHIC UNIVERSE™ · MINNEAPOLIS · NEW YORK

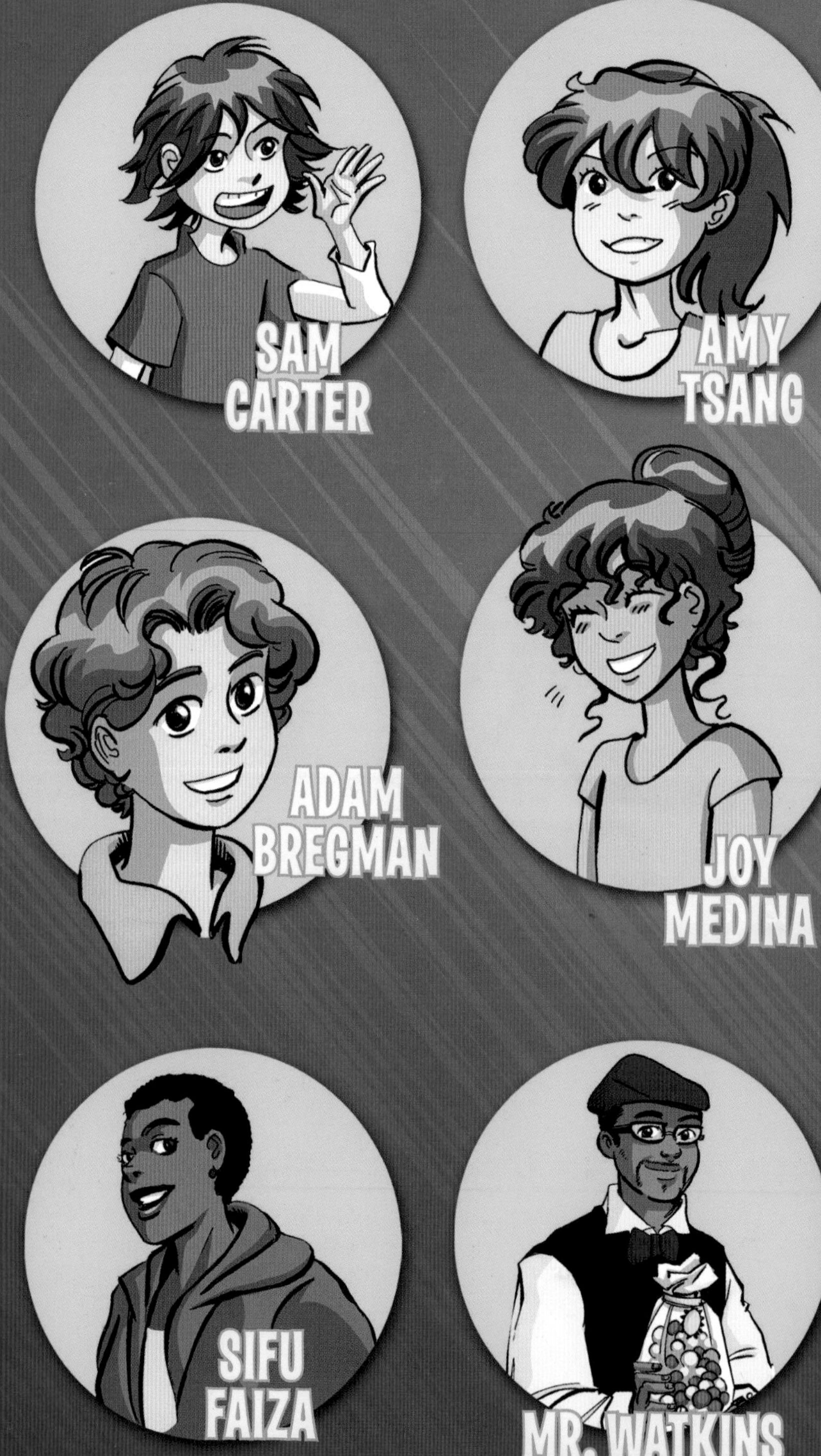
SAM CARTER
AMY TSANG
ADAM BREGMAN
JOY MEDINA
SIFU FAIZA
MR. WATKINS

THE COLONIAL HEIGHTS SOCCER TEAM

STACY LOWICKI

TOM JOHNSON

KRISTIN

MIKE

We need math when we learn how to use **money**. We can add, subtract, multiply, and divide money. Sometimes we use **decimals** when writing amounts of money. For example, if we have $35.40, we have thirty-five dollars and forty cents. The decimal separates the dollars and cents.

When we add or subtract money, it is important to line up the decimals. If the amount does not have a decimal, we can add one. For example, if we add $2.45 and $3 we can add a decimal to $3. It should look like this:

$$\begin{array}{r} \$2.45 \\ +\,\$3.00 \\ \hline \$5.45 \end{array}$$

Story by Melinda Thielbar
Pencils and inks by Tintin Pantoja
Coloring by Hi-Fi Design
Lettering by Marshall Dillon

Copyright © 2010 by Lerner Publishing Group, Inc.

Graphic Universe™ is a trademark of Lerner Publishing Group, Inc.

Graphic Universe™
A division of Lerner Publishing Group, Inc.
241 First Avenue North
Minneapolis, MN 55401 U.S.A.

Website address: www.lernerbooks.com

Library of Congress Cataloging-in-Publication Data

Thielbar, Melinda.
    The hundred-dollar robber : a mystery with money / by Melinda Thielbar ;
illustrated by Tintin Pantoja.
    p.   cm. — (Manga math mysteries)
    Summary: Someone has stolen money from the soccer team's car-wash
earnings, and the students from Sifu Faiza's Kung Fu School must set aside their
feud with the soccer players to figure out how much money was stolen and by
whom.
    ISBN: 978–0–7613–3854–3 (lib. bdg. : alk. paper)
    1. Graphic novels. [1. Graphic novels. 2. Mystery and detective stories.
3. Mathematics—Fiction. 4. Kung fu—Fiction. 5. Schools—Fiction. 6. Soccer—
Fiction.] I. Pantoja, Tintin, ill. II. Title.
PZ7.7.T48Hu 2010
741.5'973—dc22   2008053709

Manufactured in the United States of America
2 – DP – 7/15/10

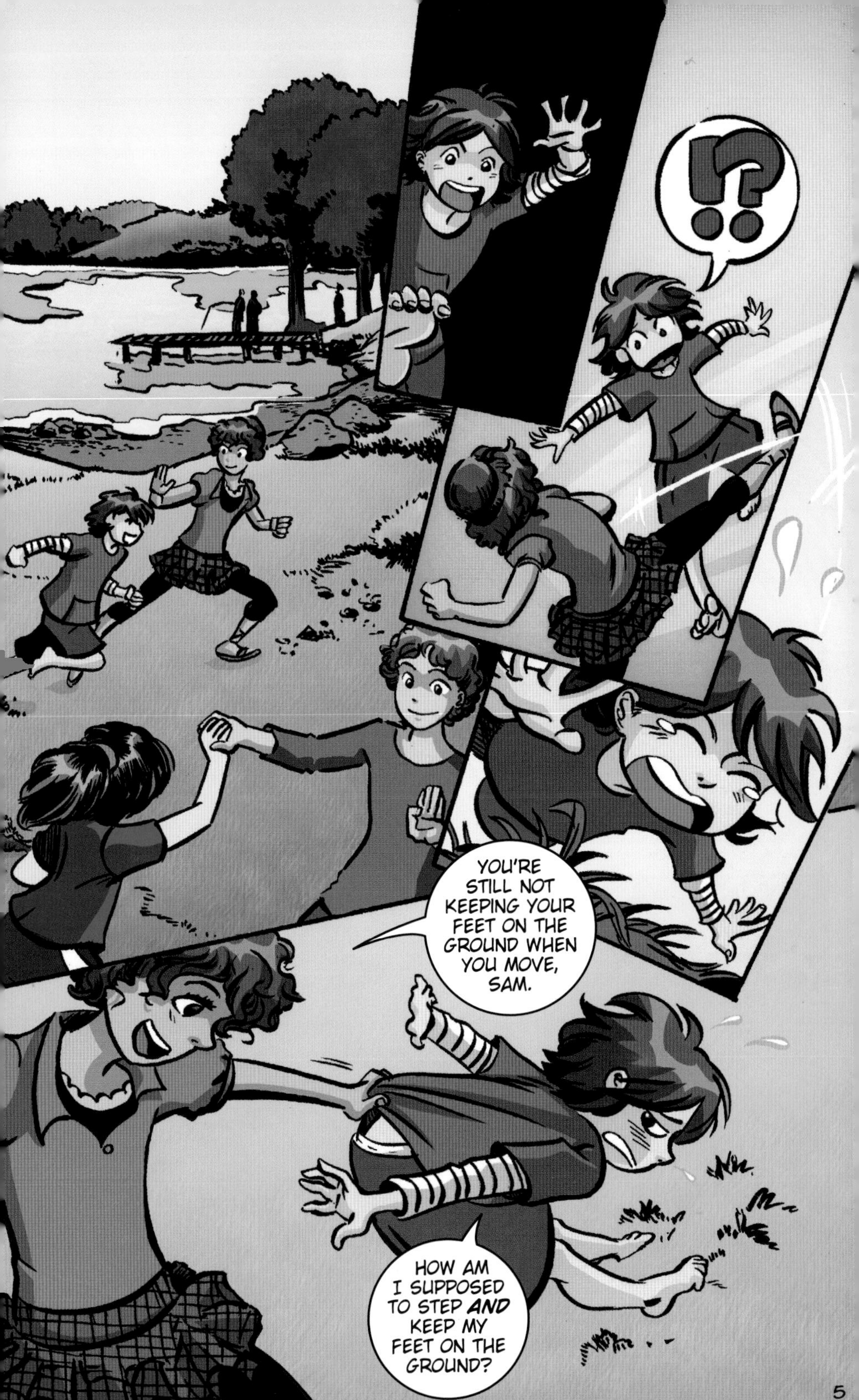

!?
YOU'RE STILL NOT KEEPING YOUR FEET ON THE GROUND WHEN YOU MOVE, SAM.
HOW AM I SUPPOSED TO STEP *AND* KEEP MY FEET ON THE GROUND?

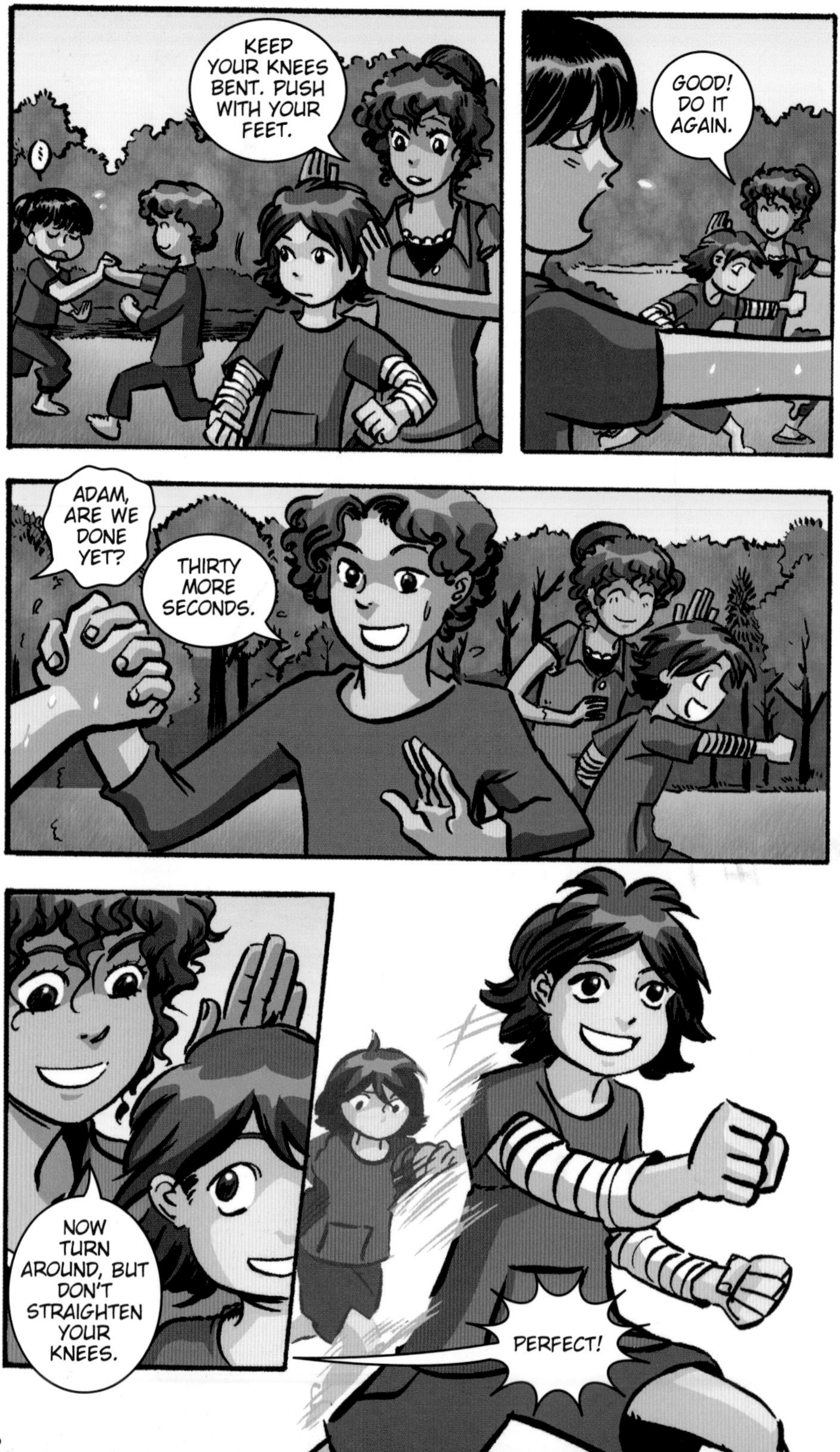
KEEP YOUR KNEES BENT. PUSH WITH YOUR FEET.
GOOD! DO IT AGAIN.
ADAM, ARE WE DONE YET?
THIRTY MORE SECONDS.
NOW TURN AROUND, BUT DON'T STRAIGHTEN YOUR KNEES.
PERFECT!

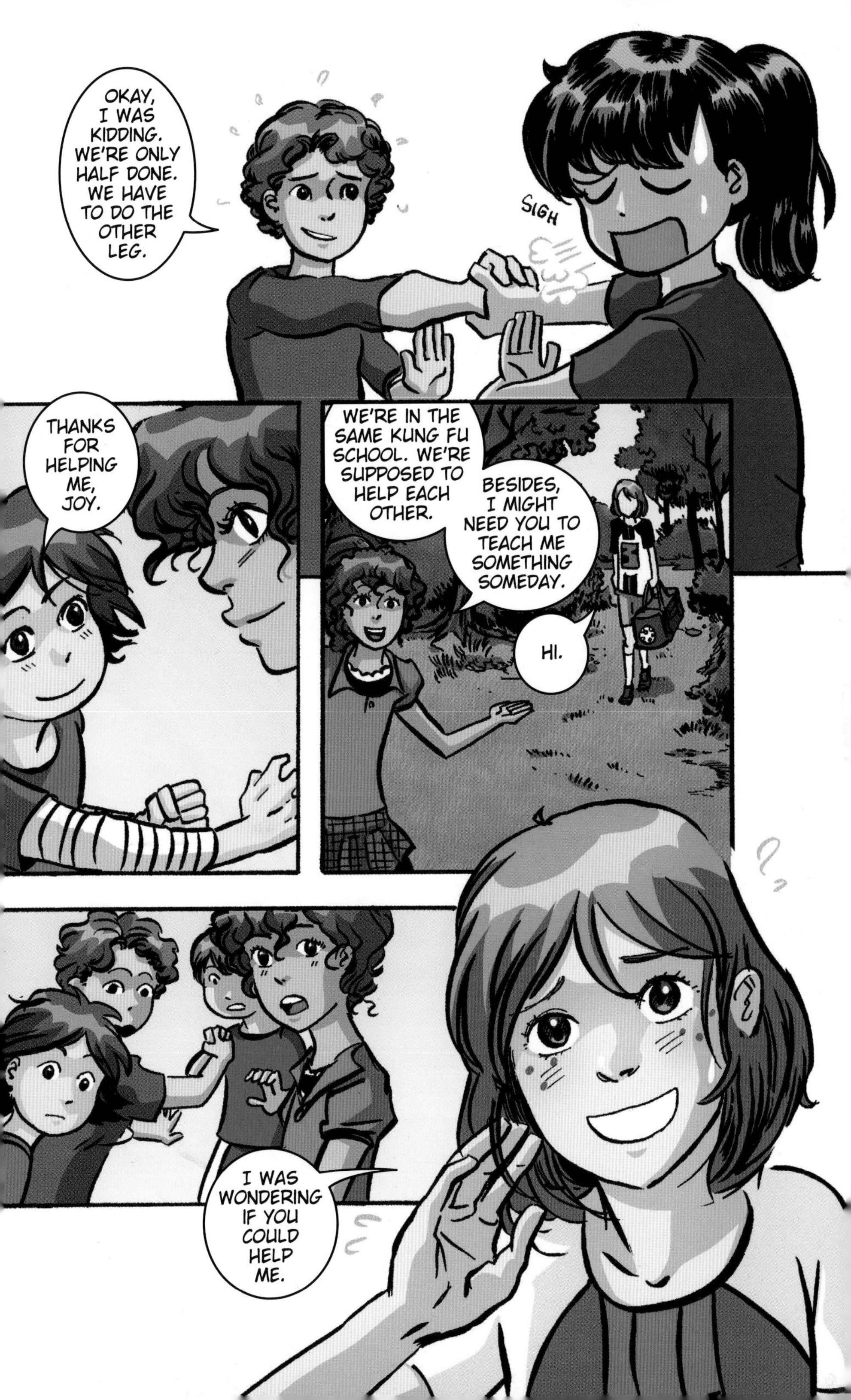
OKAY, I WAS KIDDING. WE'RE ONLY HALF DONE. WE HAVE TO DO THE OTHER LEG.
SIGH
THANKS FOR HELPING ME, JOY.
WE'RE IN THE SAME KUNG FU SCHOOL. WE'RE SUPPOSED TO HELP EACH OTHER.
BESIDES, I MIGHT NEED YOU TO TEACH ME SOMETHING SOMEDAY.
HI.
I WAS WONDERING IF YOU COULD HELP ME.

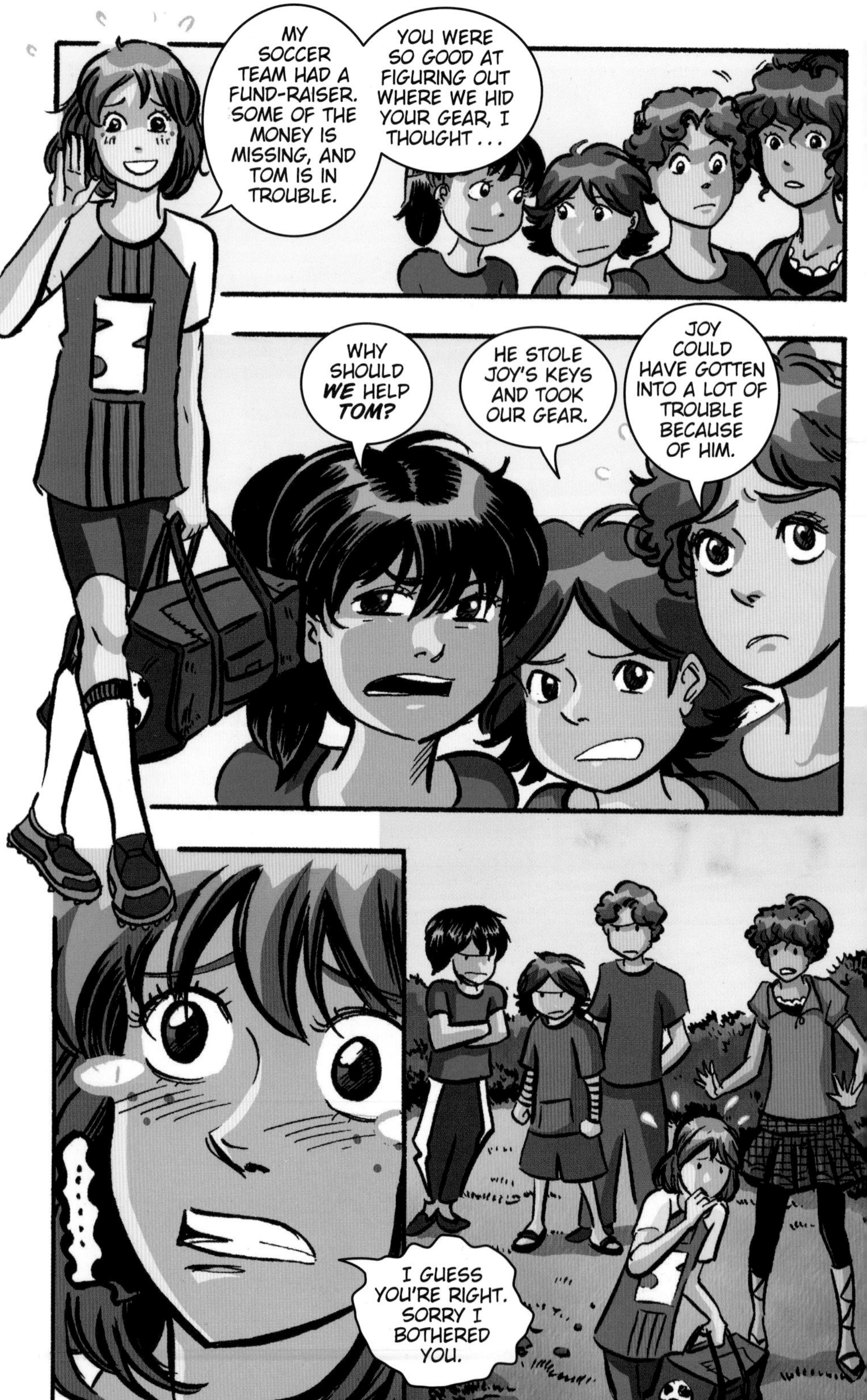
MY SOCCER TEAM HAD A FUND-RAISER. SOME OF THE MONEY IS MISSING, AND TOM IS IN TROUBLE.
YOU WERE SO GOOD AT FIGURING OUT WHERE WE HID YOUR GEAR, I THOUGHT . . .
WHY SHOULD **WE** HELP **TOM?**
HE STOLE JOY'S KEYS AND TOOK OUR GEAR.
JOY COULD HAVE GOTTEN INTO A LOT OF TROUBLE BECAUSE OF HIM.
I GUESS YOU'RE RIGHT. SORRY I BOTHERED YOU.

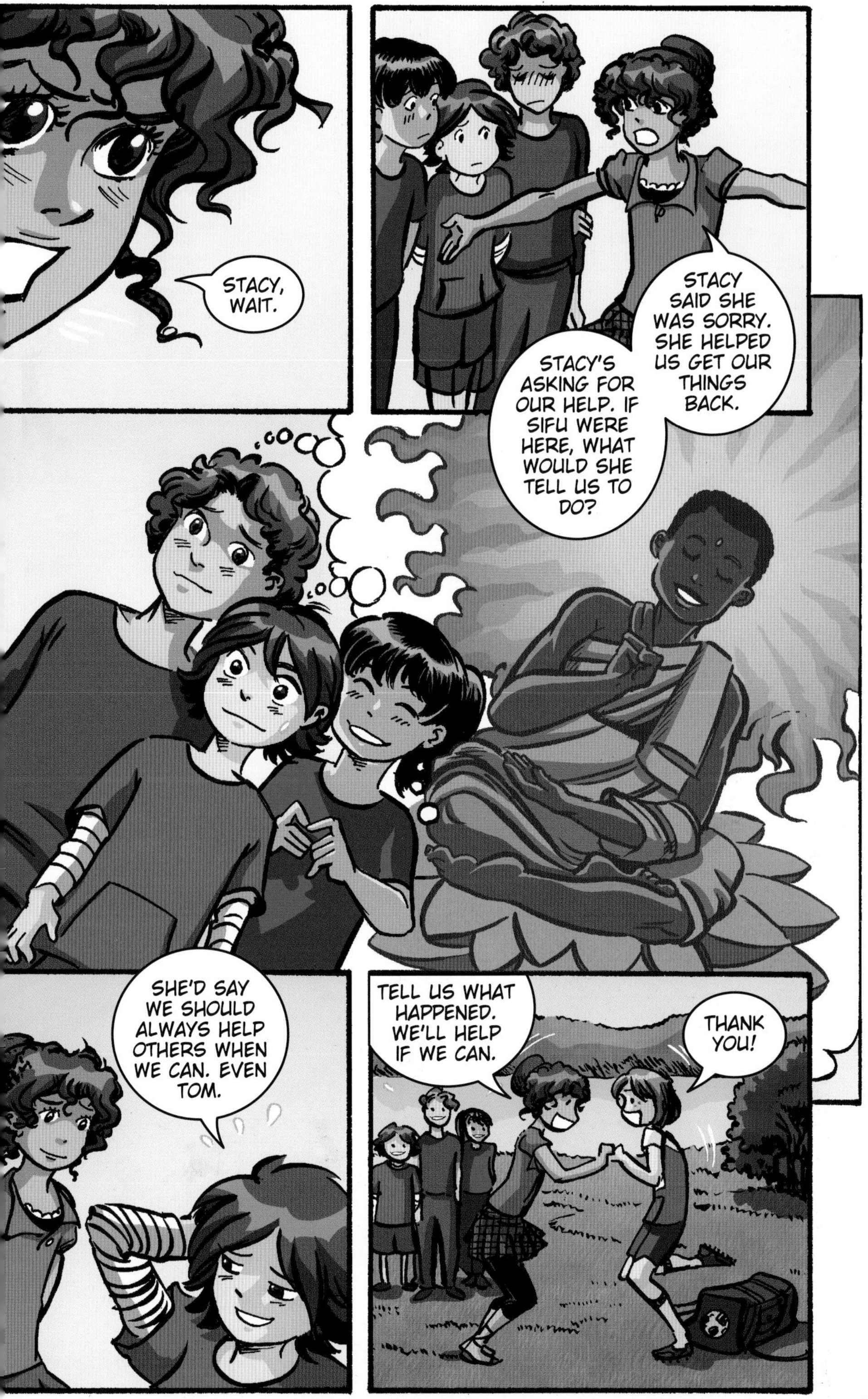
STACY, WAIT.
STACY SAID SHE WAS SORRY. SHE HELPED US GET OUR THINGS BACK.
STACY'S ASKING FOR OUR HELP. IF SIFU WERE HERE, WHAT WOULD SHE TELL US TO DO?
SHE'D SAY WE SHOULD ALWAYS HELP OTHERS WHEN WE CAN. EVEN TOM.
TELL US WHAT HAPPENED. WE'LL HELP IF WE CAN.
THANK YOU!

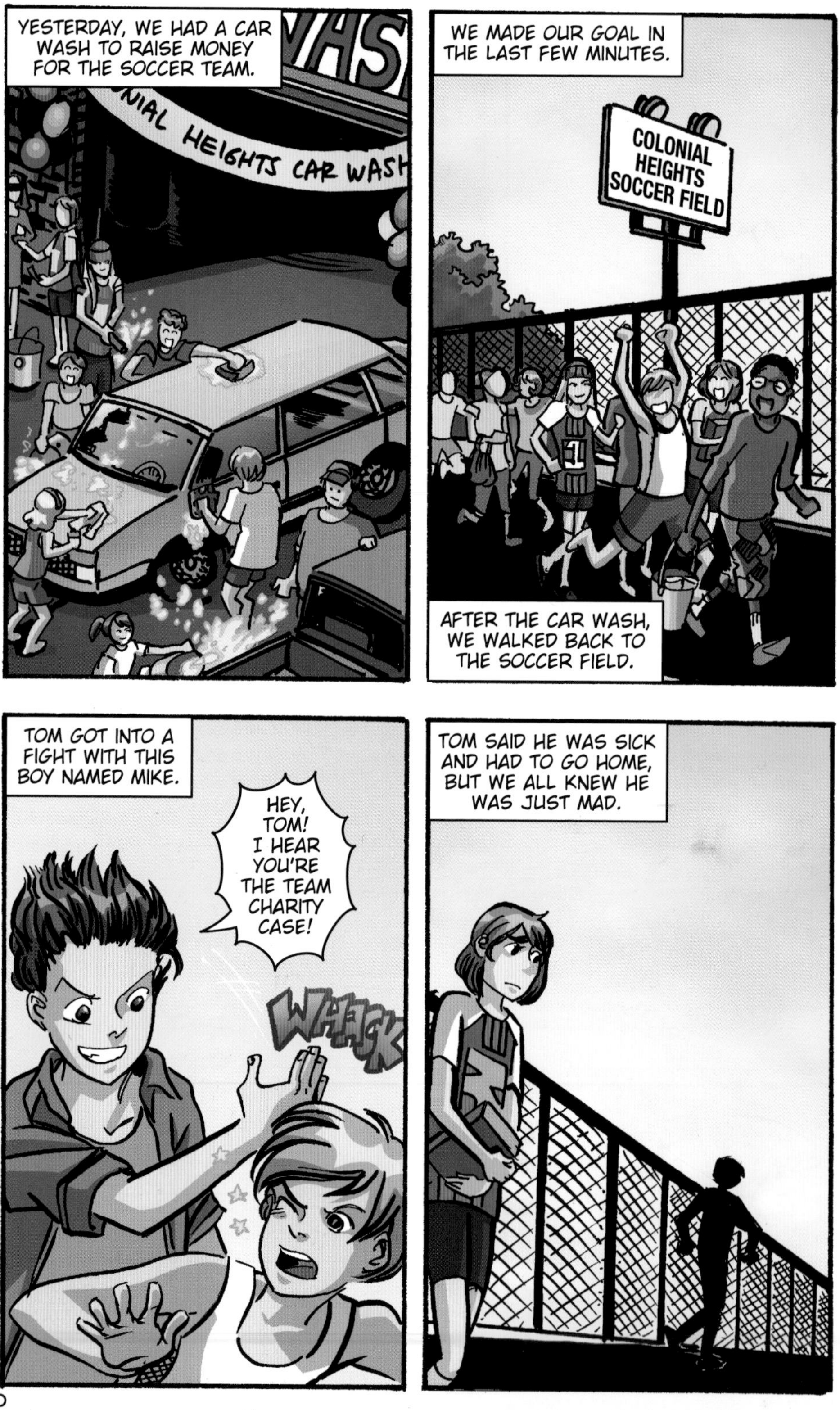
YESTERDAY, WE HAD A CAR WASH TO RAISE MONEY FOR THE SOCCER TEAM.
HEIGHTS CAR WASH
WE MADE OUR GOAL IN THE LAST FEW MINUTES.
COLONIAL HEIGHTS SOCCER FIELD
AFTER THE CAR WASH, WE WALKED BACK TO THE SOCCER FIELD.
TOM GOT INTO A FIGHT WITH THIS BOY NAMED MIKE.
HEY, TOM! I HEAR YOU'RE THE TEAM CHARITY CASE!
WHACK
TOM SAID HE WAS SICK AND HAD TO GO HOME, BUT WE ALL KNEW HE WAS JUST MAD.

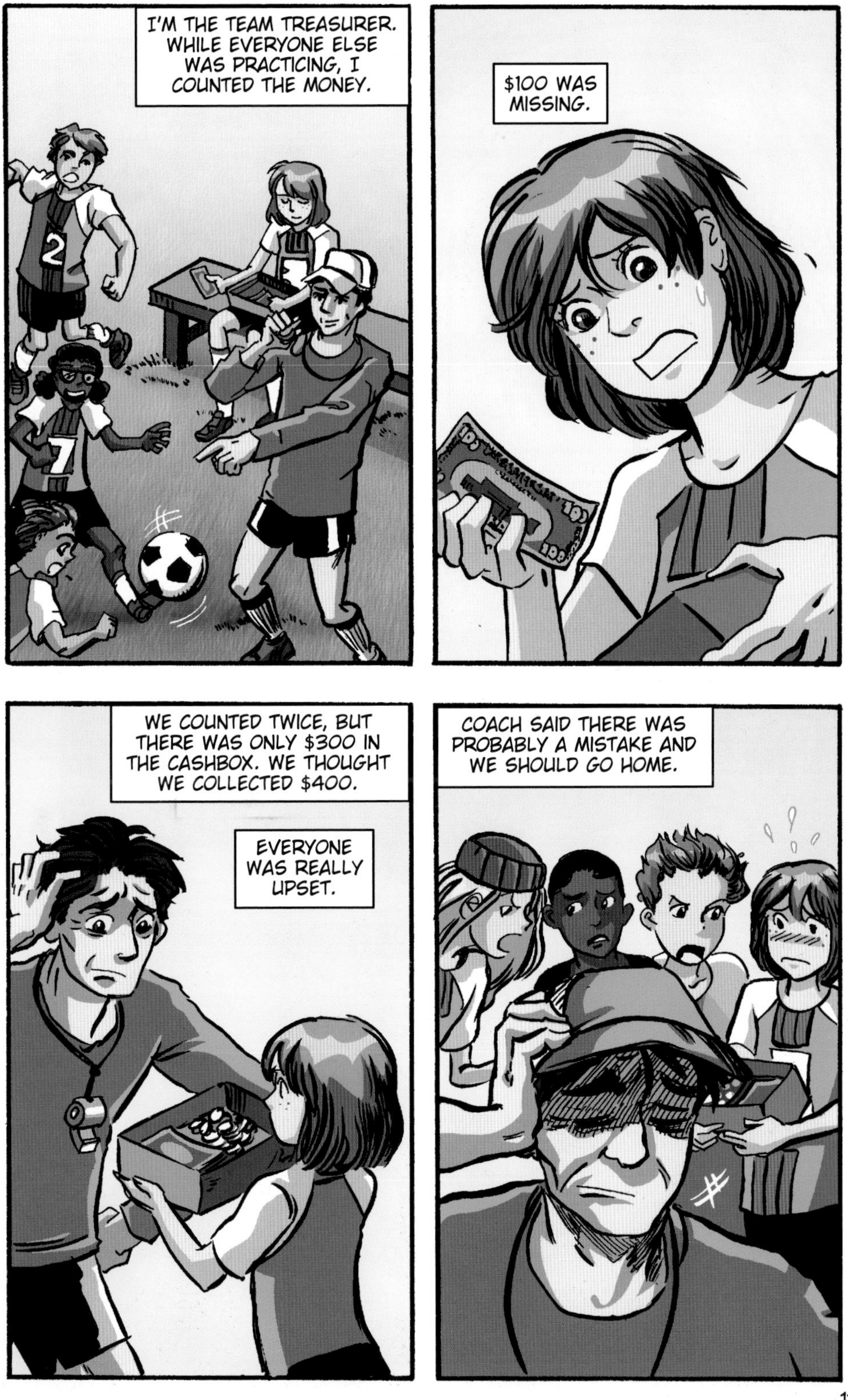
I'M THE TEAM TREASURER. WHILE EVERYONE ELSE WAS PRACTICING, I COUNTED THE MONEY.
$100 WAS MISSING.
WE COUNTED TWICE, BUT THERE WAS ONLY $300 IN THE CASHBOX. WE THOUGHT WE COLLECTED $400.
EVERYONE WAS REALLY UPSET.
COACH SAID THERE WAS PROBABLY A MISTAKE AND WE SHOULD GO HOME.

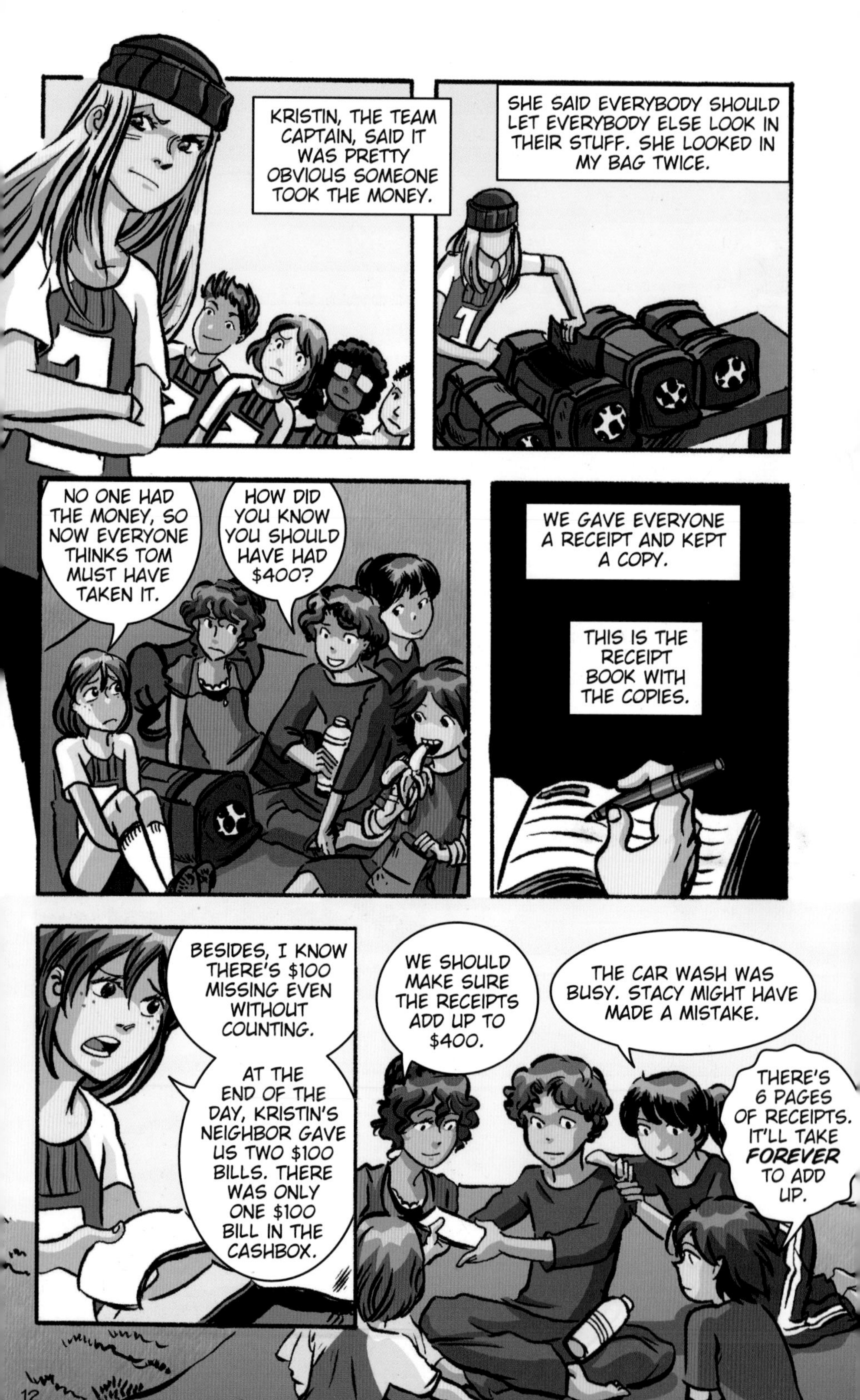

KRISTIN, THE TEAM CAPTAIN, SAID IT WAS PRETTY OBVIOUS SOMEONE TOOK THE MONEY.
SHE SAID EVERYBODY SHOULD LET EVERYBODY ELSE LOOK IN THEIR STUFF. SHE LOOKED IN MY BAG TWICE.
NO ONE HAD THE MONEY, SO NOW EVERYONE THINKS TOM MUST HAVE TAKEN IT.
HOW DID YOU KNOW YOU SHOULD HAVE HAD $400?
WE GAVE EVERYONE A RECEIPT AND KEPT A COPY.
THIS IS THE RECEIPT BOOK WITH THE COPIES.
BESIDES, I KNOW THERE'S $100 MISSING EVEN WITHOUT COUNTING.
AT THE END OF THE DAY, KRISTIN'S NEIGHBOR GAVE US TWO $100 BILLS. THERE WAS ONLY ONE $100 BILL IN THE CASHBOX.
WE SHOULD MAKE SURE THE RECEIPTS ADD UP TO $400.
THE CAR WASH WAS BUSY. STACY MIGHT HAVE MADE A MISTAKE.
THERE'S 6 PAGES OF RECEIPTS. IT'LL TAKE ***FOREVER*** TO ADD UP.

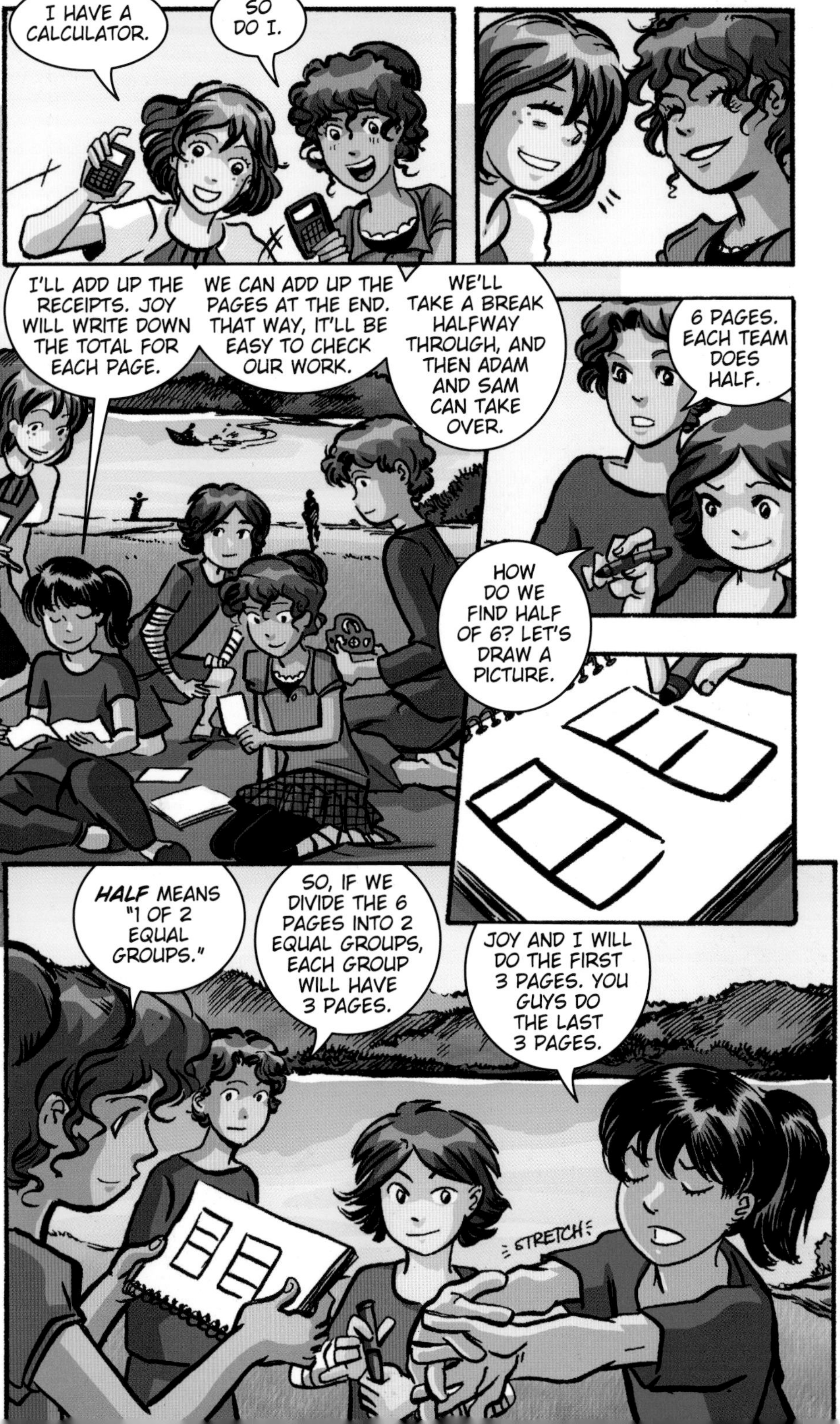
I HAVE A CALCULATOR.
SO DO I.
I'LL ADD UP THE RECEIPTS. JOY WILL WRITE DOWN THE TOTAL FOR EACH PAGE.
WE CAN ADD UP THE PAGES AT THE END. THAT WAY, IT'LL BE EASY TO CHECK OUR WORK.
WE'LL TAKE A BREAK HALFWAY THROUGH, AND THEN ADAM AND SAM CAN TAKE OVER.
6 PAGES. EACH TEAM DOES HALF.
HOW DO WE FIND HALF OF 6? LET'S DRAW A PICTURE.
HALF MEANS "1 OF 2 EQUAL GROUPS."
SO, IF WE DIVIDE THE 6 PAGES INTO 2 EQUAL GROUPS, EACH GROUP WILL HAVE 3 PAGES.
JOY AND I WILL DO THE FIRST 3 PAGES. YOU GUYS DO THE LAST 3 PAGES.
STRETCH

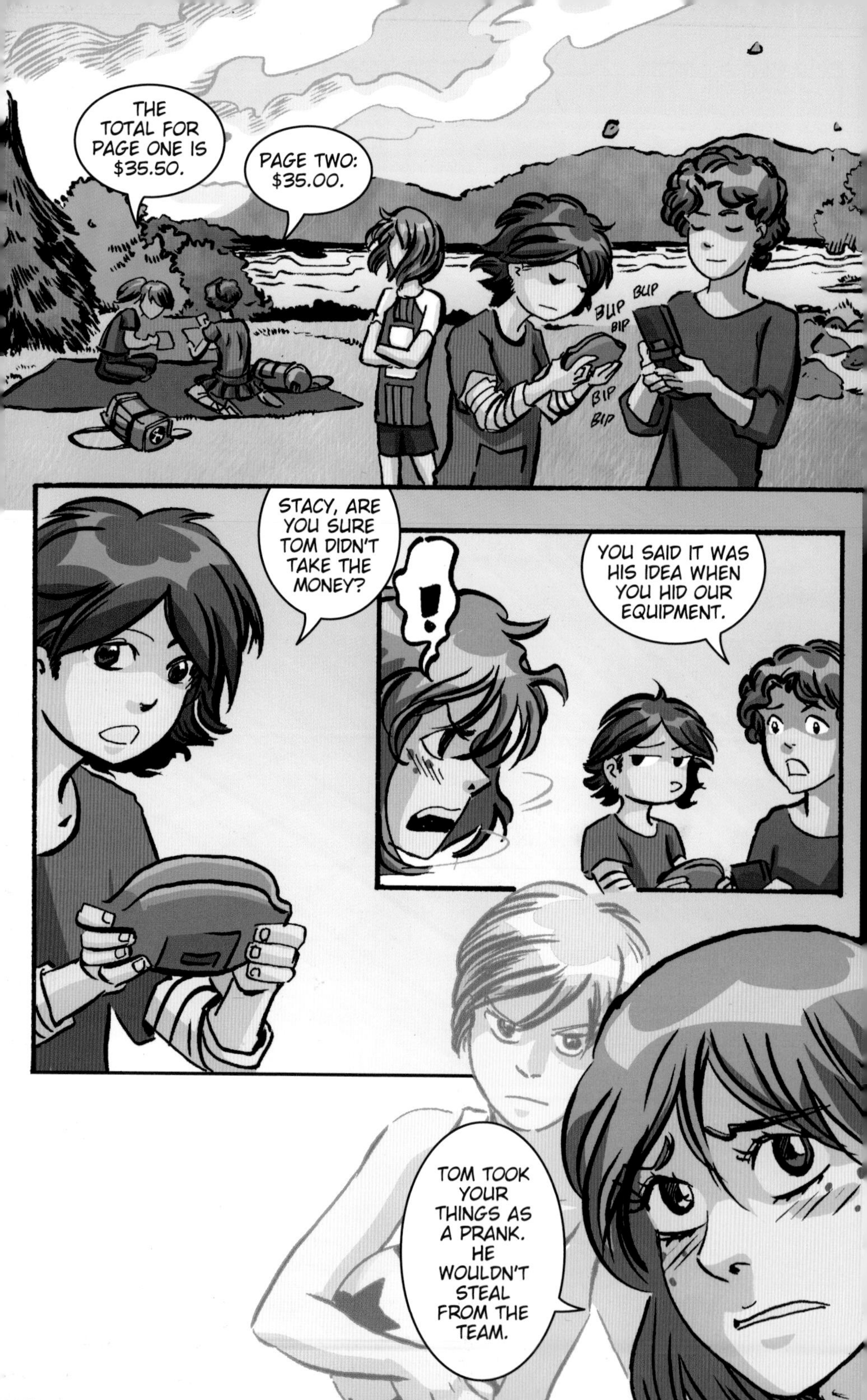
THE TOTAL FOR PAGE ONE IS $35.50.
PAGE TWO: $35.00.
BUP BUP
BIP
BIP
BIP
STACY, ARE YOU SURE TOM DIDN'T TAKE THE MONEY?
!
YOU SAID IT WAS HIS IDEA WHEN YOU HID OUR EQUIPMENT.
TOM TOOK YOUR THINGS AS A PRANK. HE WOULDN'T STEAL FROM THE TEAM.

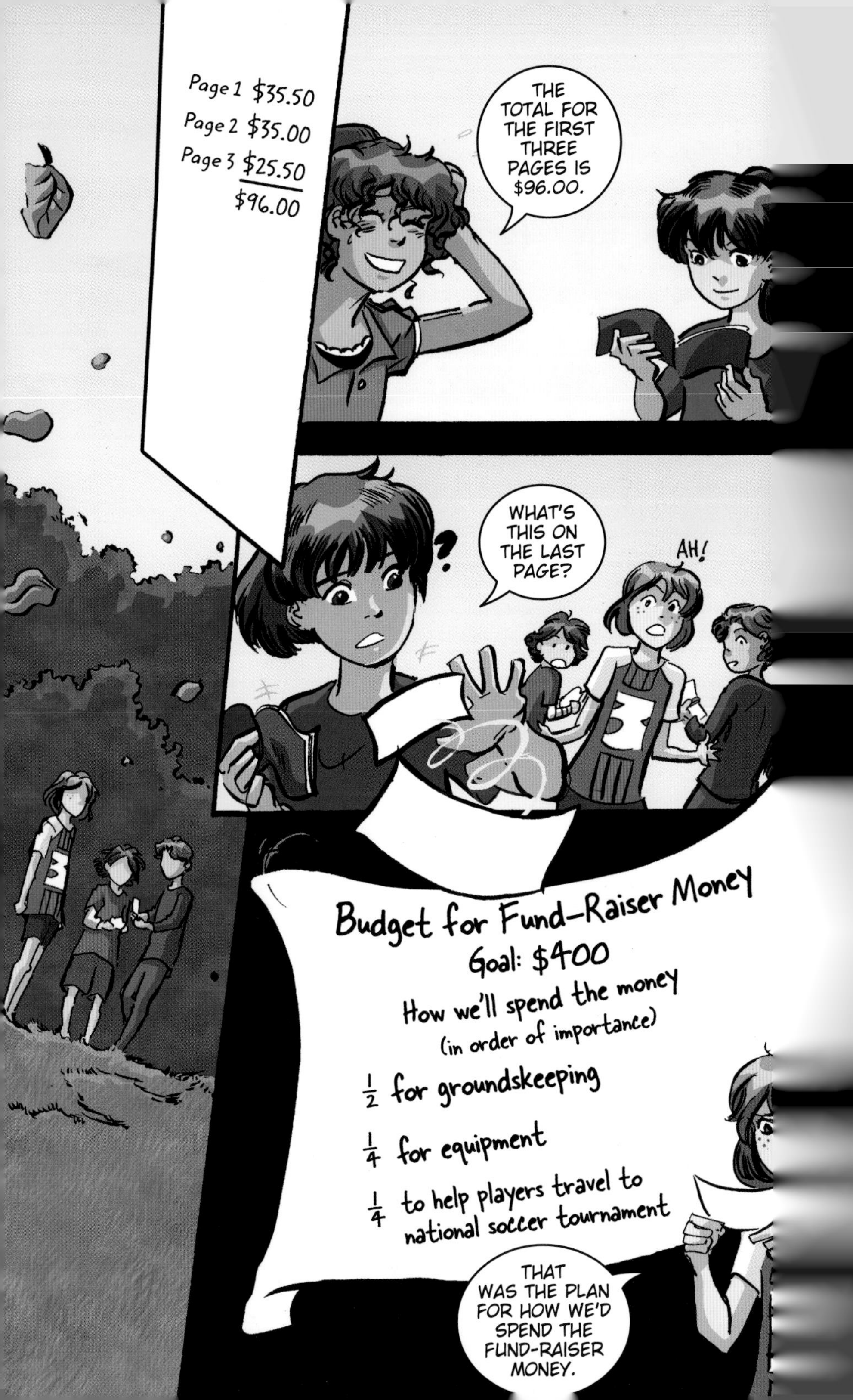
Page 1 $35.50
Page 2 $35.00
Page 3 $25.50
$96.00
THE TOTAL FOR THE FIRST THREE PAGES IS $96.00.
WHAT'S THIS ON THE LAST PAGE?
AH!
Budget for Fund-Raiser Money
Goal: $400
How we'll spend the money
(in order of importance)
1/2 for groundskeeping
1/4 for equipment
1/4 to help players travel to national soccer tournament
THAT WAS THE PLAN FOR HOW WE'D SPEND THE FUND-RAISER MONEY.

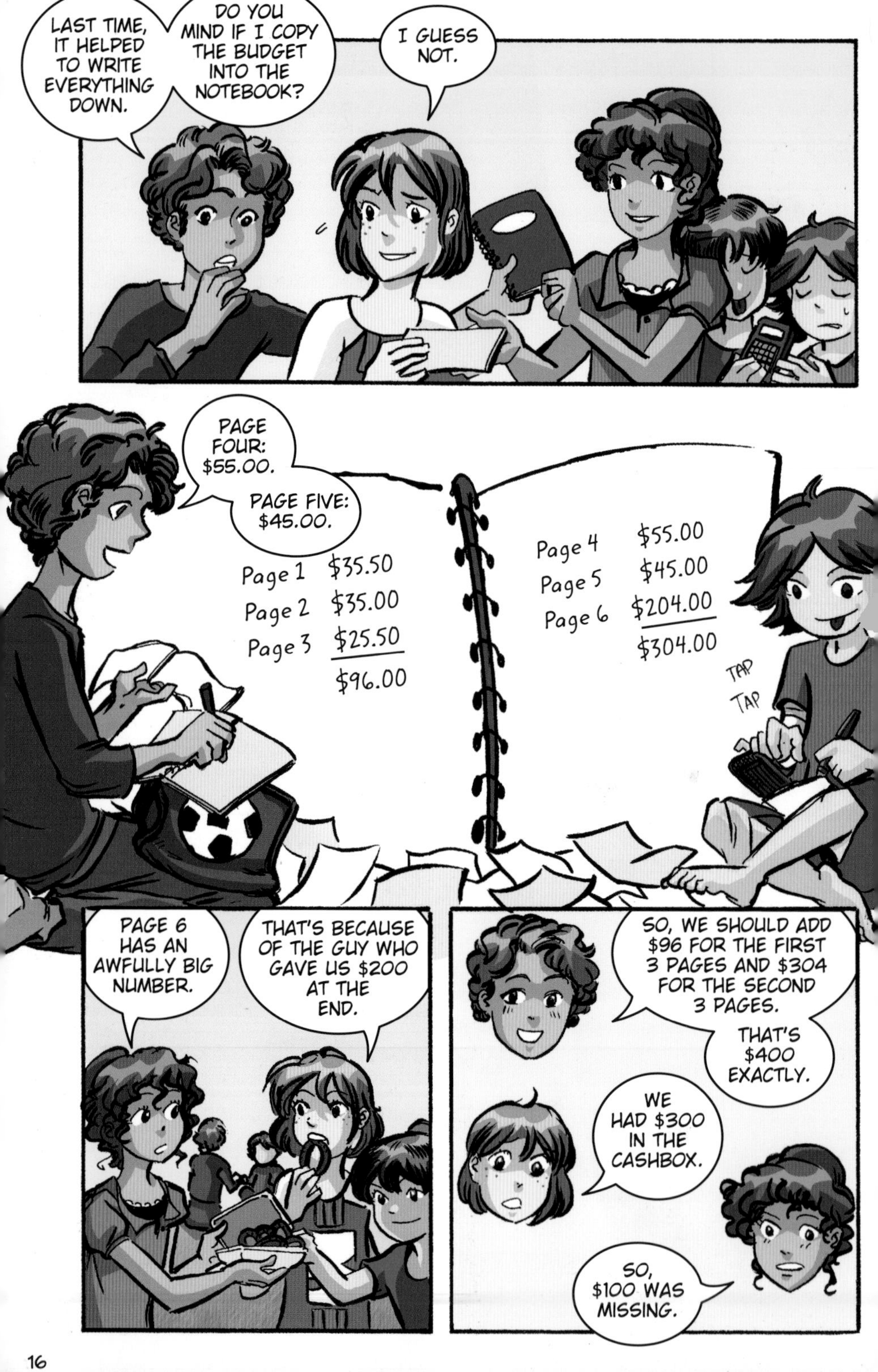

LAST TIME, IT HELPED TO WRITE EVERYTHING DOWN.
DO YOU MIND IF I COPY THE BUDGET INTO THE NOTEBOOK?
I GUESS NOT.
PAGE FOUR: $55.00.
PAGE FIVE: $45.00.
Page 1 $35.50
Page 2 $35.00
Page 3 $25.50
$96.00
Page 4 $55.00
Page 5 $45.00
Page 6 $204.00
$304.00
TAP TAP
PAGE 6 HAS AN AWFULLY BIG NUMBER.
THAT'S BECAUSE OF THE GUY WHO GAVE US $200 AT THE END.
SO, WE SHOULD ADD $96 FOR THE FIRST 3 PAGES AND $304 FOR THE SECOND 3 PAGES.
THAT'S $400 EXACTLY.
WE HAD $300 IN THE CASHBOX.
SO, $100 WAS MISSING.

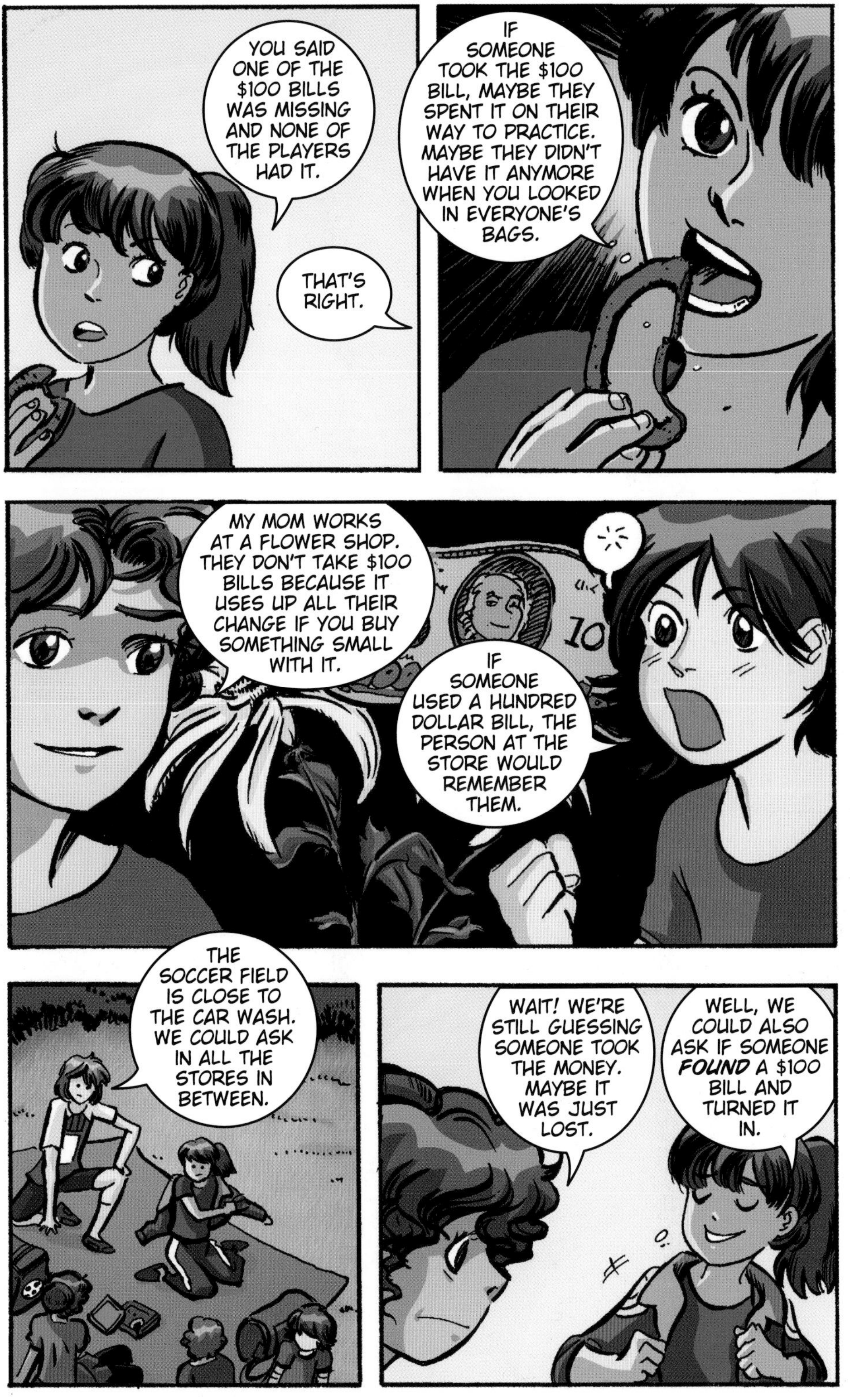
YOU SAID ONE OF THE $100 BILLS WAS MISSING AND NONE OF THE PLAYERS HAD IT.
THAT'S RIGHT.
IF SOMEONE TOOK THE $100 BILL, MAYBE THEY SPENT IT ON THEIR WAY TO PRACTICE. MAYBE THEY DIDN'T HAVE IT ANYMORE WHEN YOU LOOKED IN EVERYONE'S BAGS.
MY MOM WORKS AT A FLOWER SHOP. THEY DON'T TAKE $100 BILLS BECAUSE IT USES UP ALL THEIR CHANGE IF YOU BUY SOMETHING SMALL WITH IT.
IF SOMEONE USED A HUNDRED DOLLAR BILL, THE PERSON AT THE STORE WOULD REMEMBER THEM.
THE SOCCER FIELD IS CLOSE TO THE CAR WASH. WE COULD ASK IN ALL THE STORES IN BETWEEN.
WAIT! WE'RE STILL GUESSING SOMEONE TOOK THE MONEY. MAYBE IT WAS JUST LOST.
WELL, WE COULD ALSO ASK IF SOMEONE *FOUND* A $100 BILL AND TURNED IT IN.

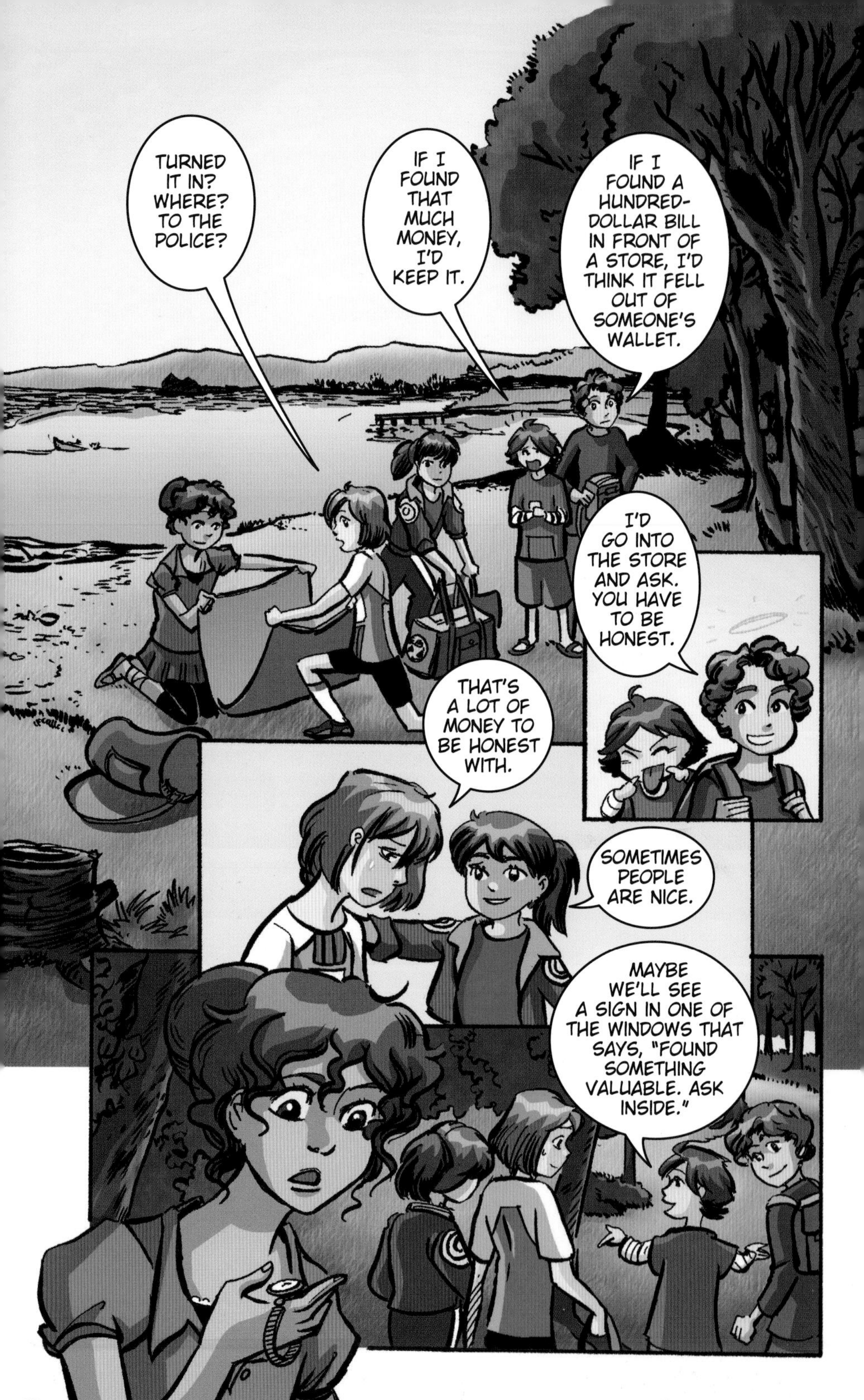
TURNED IT IN? WHERE? TO THE POLICE?
IF I FOUND THAT MUCH MONEY, I'D KEEP IT.
IF I FOUND A HUNDRED-DOLLAR BILL IN FRONT OF A STORE, I'D THINK IT FELL OUT OF SOMEONE'S WALLET.
I'D GO INTO THE STORE AND ASK. YOU HAVE TO BE HONEST.
THAT'S A LOT OF MONEY TO BE HONEST WITH.
SOMETIMES PEOPLE ARE NICE.
MAYBE WE'LL SEE A SIGN IN ONE OF THE WINDOWS THAT SAYS, "FOUND SOMETHING VALUABLE. ASK INSIDE."

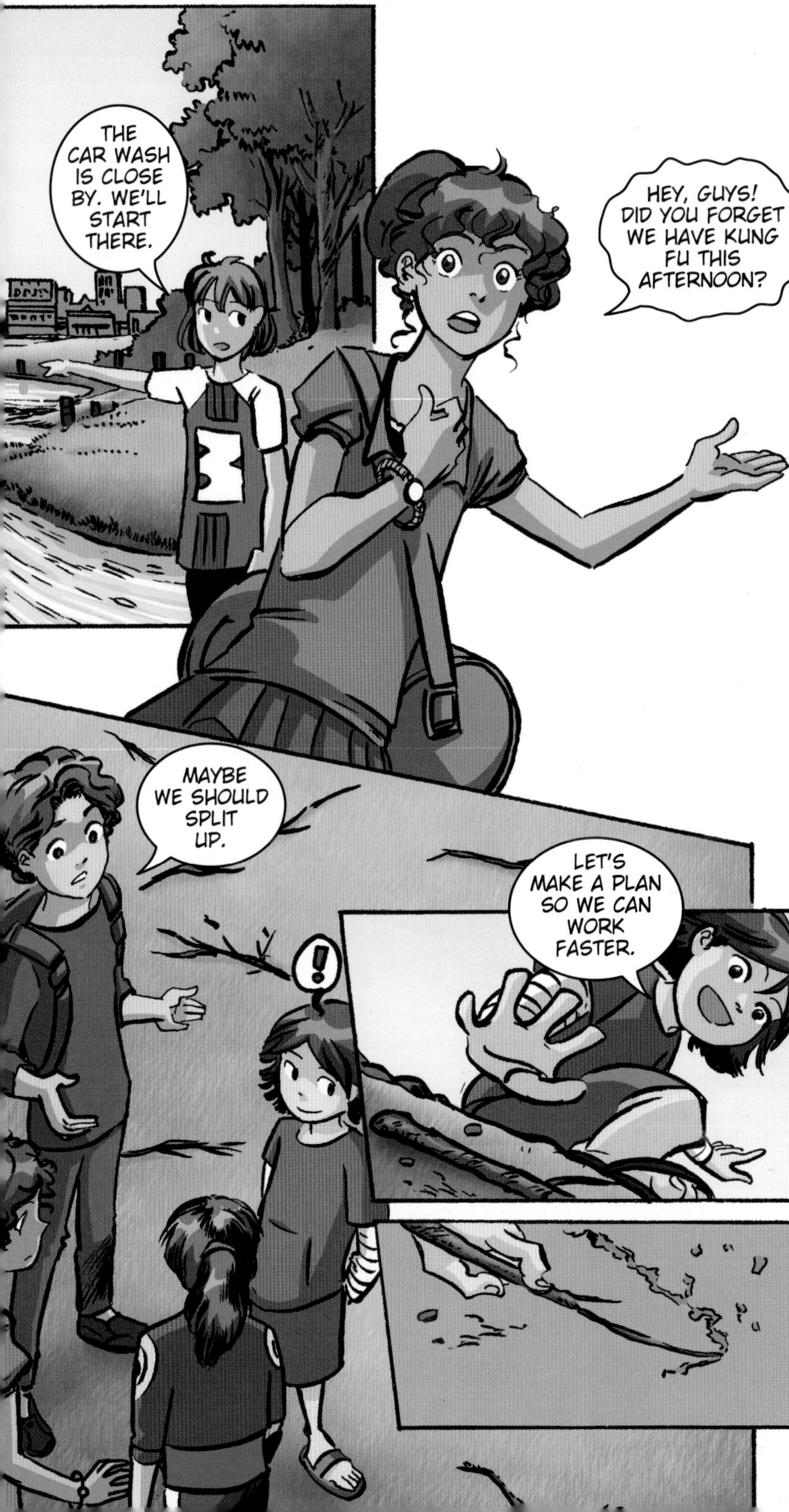
THE CAR WASH IS CLOSE BY. WE'LL START THERE.
HEY, GUYS! DID YOU FORGET WE HAVE KUNG FU THIS AFTERNOON?
MAYBE WE SHOULD SPLIT UP.
!
LET'S MAKE A PLAN SO WE CAN WORK FASTER.

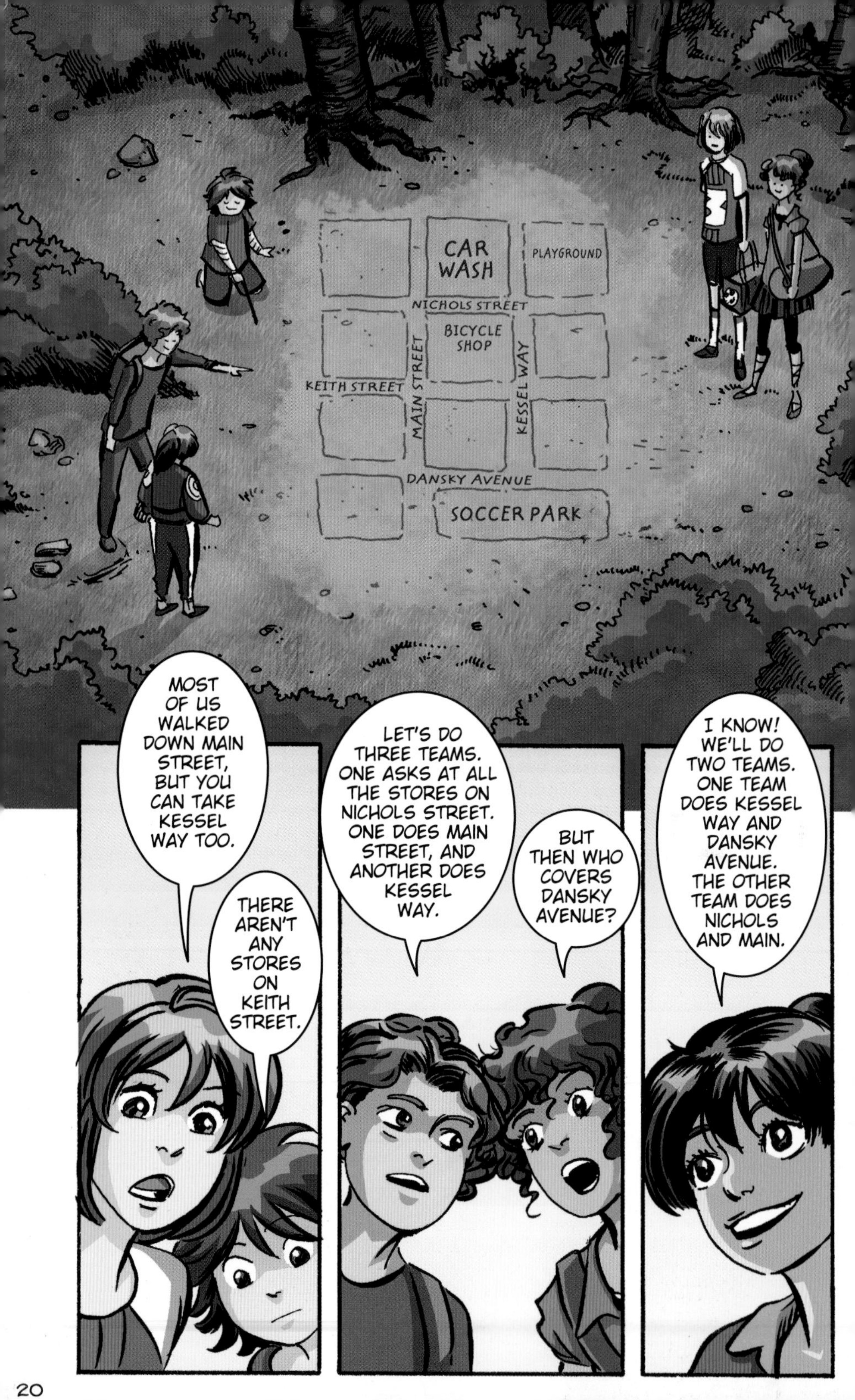
CAR WASH
PLAYGROUND
NICHOLS STREET
BICYCLE SHOP
KEITH STREET
MAIN STREET
KESSEL WAY
DANSKY AVENUE
SOCCER PARK
MOST OF US WALKED DOWN MAIN STREET, BUT YOU CAN TAKE KESSEL WAY TOO.
THERE AREN'T ANY STORES ON KEITH STREET.
LET'S DO THREE TEAMS. ONE ASKS AT ALL THE STORES ON NICHOLS STREET. ONE DOES MAIN STREET, AND ANOTHER DOES KESSEL WAY.
BUT THEN WHO COVERS DANSKY AVENUE?
I KNOW! WE'LL DO TWO TEAMS. ONE TEAM DOES KESSEL WAY AND DANSKY AVENUE. THE OTHER TEAM DOES NICHOLS AND MAIN.

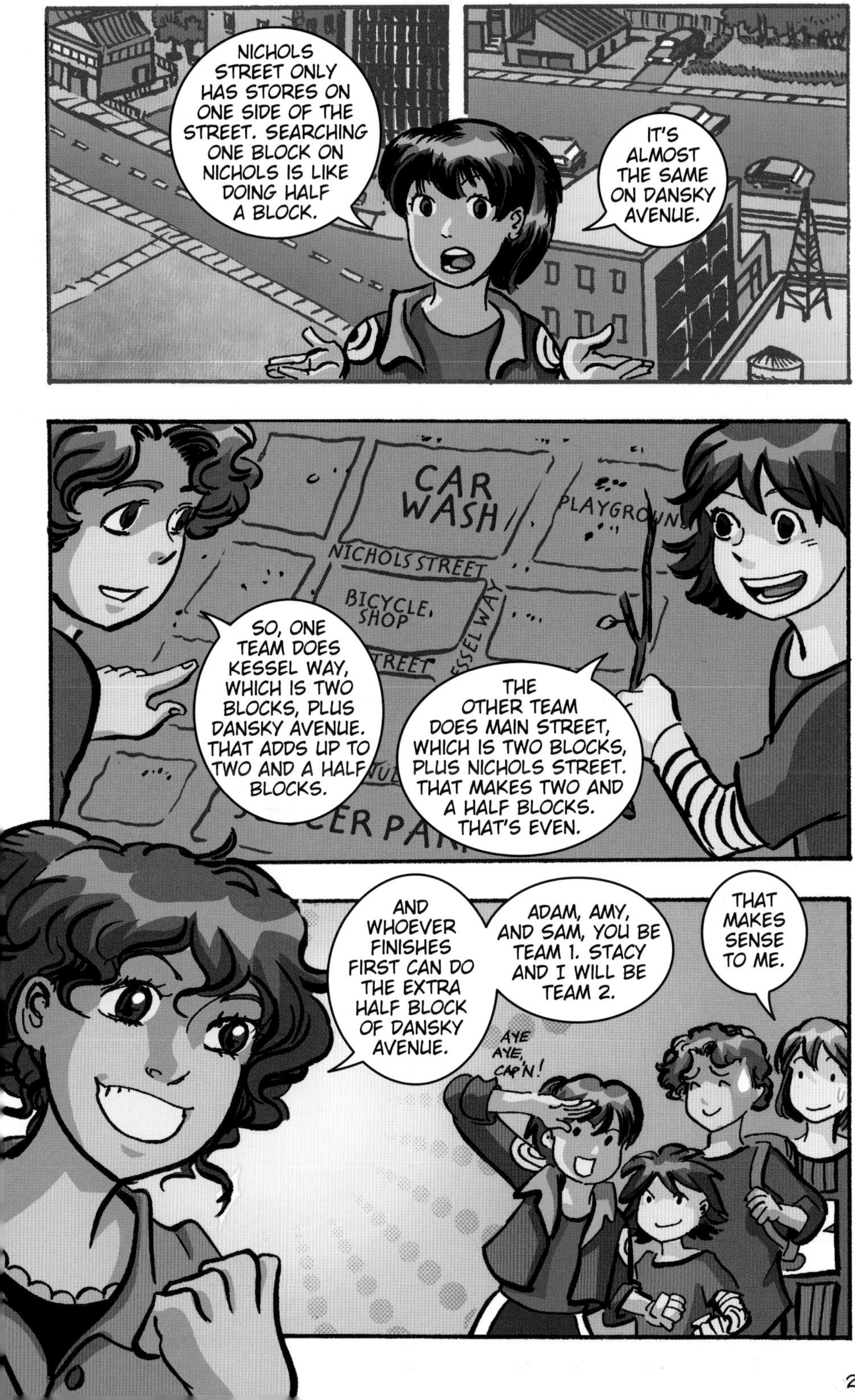
NICHOLS STREET ONLY HAS STORES ON ONE SIDE OF THE STREET. SEARCHING ONE BLOCK ON NICHOLS IS LIKE DOING HALF A BLOCK.
IT'S ALMOST THE SAME ON DANSKY AVENUE.
CAR WASH
PLAYGROUN
NICHOLS STREET
BICYCLE SHOP
SO, ONE TEAM DOES KESSEL WAY, WHICH IS TWO BLOCKS, PLUS DANSKY AVENUE. THAT ADDS UP TO TWO AND A HALF BLOCKS.
THE OTHER TEAM DOES MAIN STREET, WHICH IS TWO BLOCKS, PLUS NICHOLS STREET. THAT MAKES TWO AND A HALF BLOCKS. THAT'S EVEN.
AND WHOEVER FINISHES FIRST CAN DO THE EXTRA HALF BLOCK OF DANSKY AVENUE.
ADAM, AMY, AND SAM, YOU BE TEAM 1. STACY AND I WILL BE TEAM 2.
THAT MAKES SENSE TO ME.
AYE AYE, CAP'N!

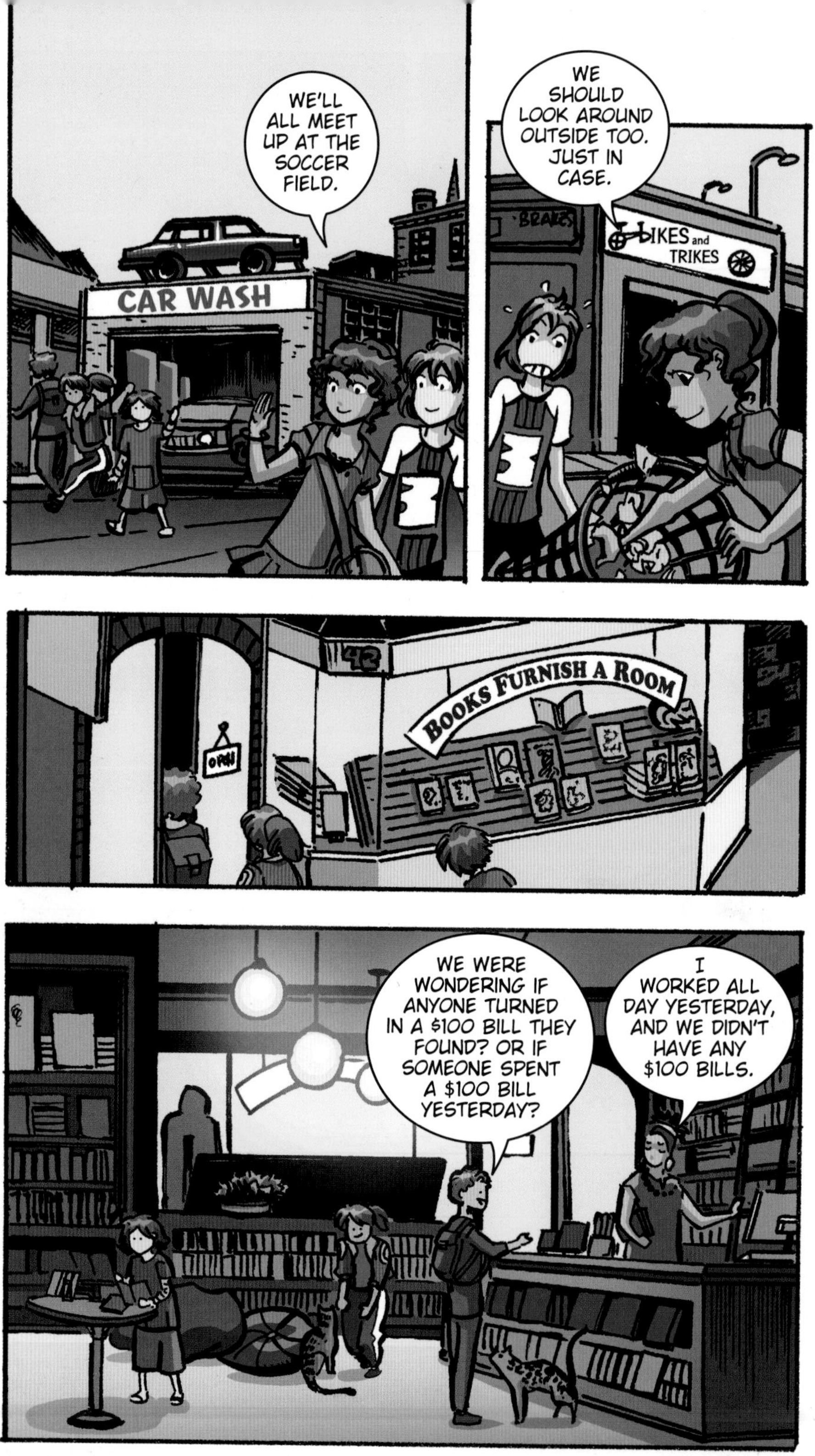
WE'LL ALL MEET UP AT THE SOCCER FIELD.
CAR WASH
WE SHOULD LOOK AROUND OUTSIDE TOO. JUST IN CASE.
BRAKES
BIKES and TRIKES
42
BOOKS FURNISH A ROOM
OPEN
WE WERE WONDERING IF ANYONE TURNED IN A $100 BILL THEY FOUND? OR IF SOMEONE SPENT A $100 BILL YESTERDAY?
I WORKED ALL DAY YESTERDAY, AND WE DIDN'T HAVE ANY $100 BILLS.

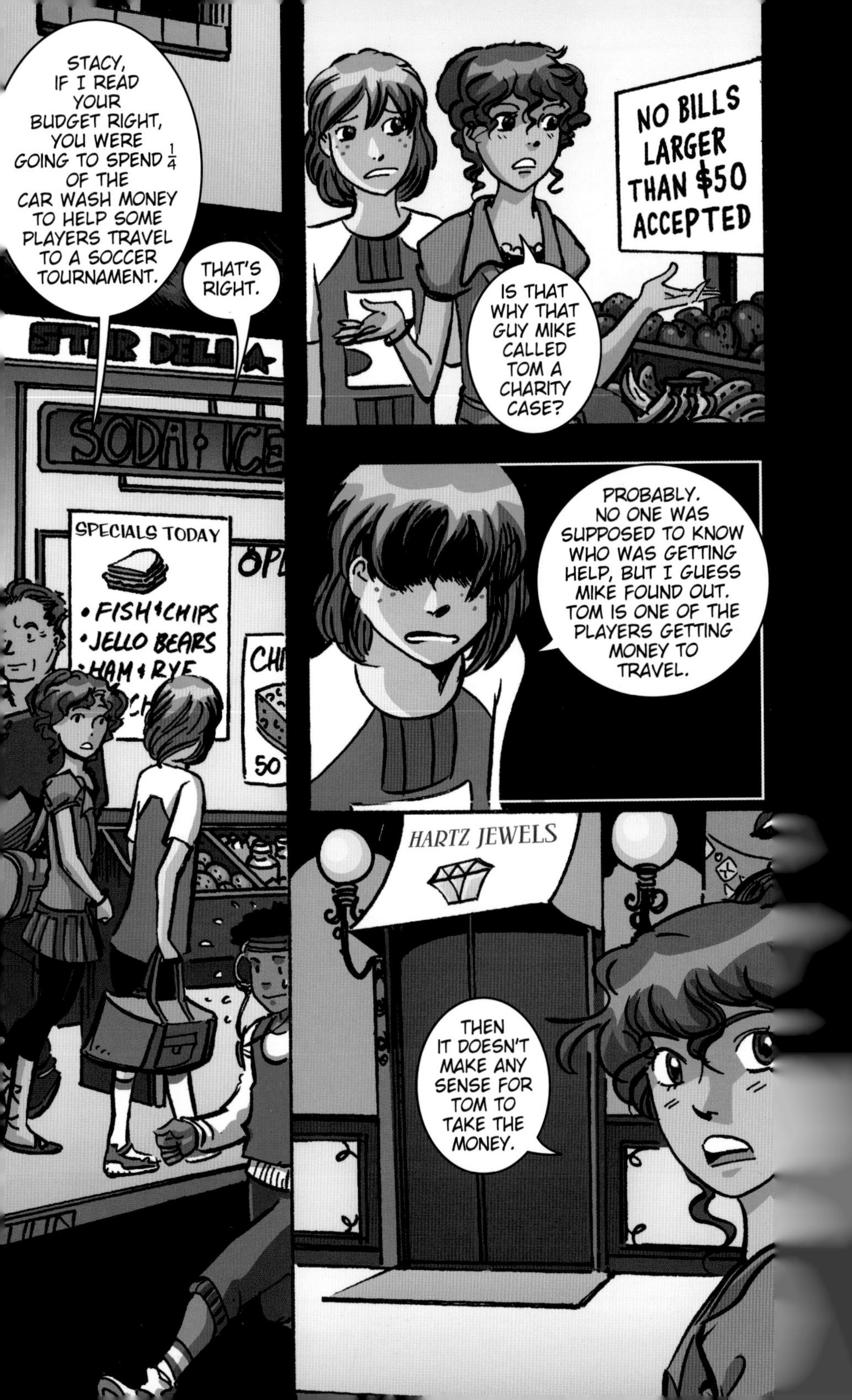
STACY, IF I READ YOUR BUDGET RIGHT, YOU WERE GOING TO SPEND $\frac{1}{4}$ OF THE CAR WASH MONEY TO HELP SOME PLAYERS TRAVEL TO A SOCCER TOURNAMENT.
THAT'S RIGHT.
SPECIALS TODAY
• FISH & CHIPS
• JELLO BEARS
• HAM & RYE
NO BILLS LARGER THAN $50 ACCEPTED
IS THAT WHY THAT GUY MIKE CALLED TOM A CHARITY CASE?
PROBABLY. NO ONE WAS SUPPOSED TO KNOW WHO WAS GETTING HELP, BUT I GUESS MIKE FOUND OUT. TOM IS ONE OF THE PLAYERS GETTING MONEY TO TRAVEL.
HARTZ JEWELS
THEN IT DOESN'T MAKE ANY SENSE FOR TOM TO TAKE THE MONEY.

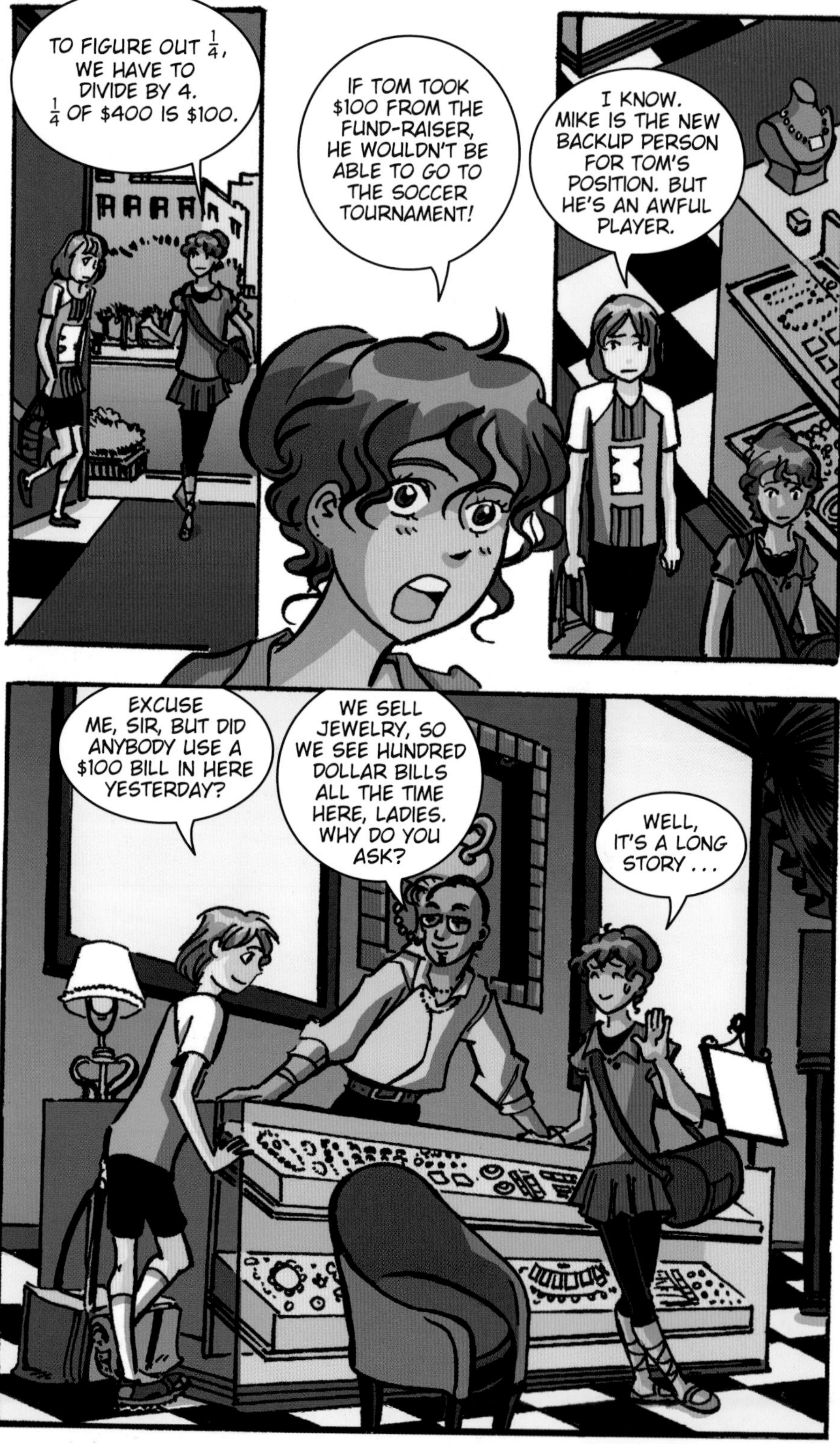
TO FIGURE OUT $\frac{1}{4}$, WE HAVE TO DIVIDE BY 4. $\frac{1}{4}$ OF $400 IS $100.
IF TOM TOOK $100 FROM THE FUND-RAISER, HE WOULDN'T BE ABLE TO GO TO THE SOCCER TOURNAMENT!
I KNOW. MIKE IS THE NEW BACKUP PERSON FOR TOM'S POSITION. BUT HE'S AN AWFUL PLAYER.
EXCUSE ME, SIR, BUT DID ANYBODY USE A $100 BILL IN HERE YESTERDAY?
WE SELL JEWELRY, SO WE SEE HUNDRED DOLLAR BILLS ALL THE TIME HERE, LADIES. WHY DO YOU ASK?
WELL, IT'S A LONG STORY . . .

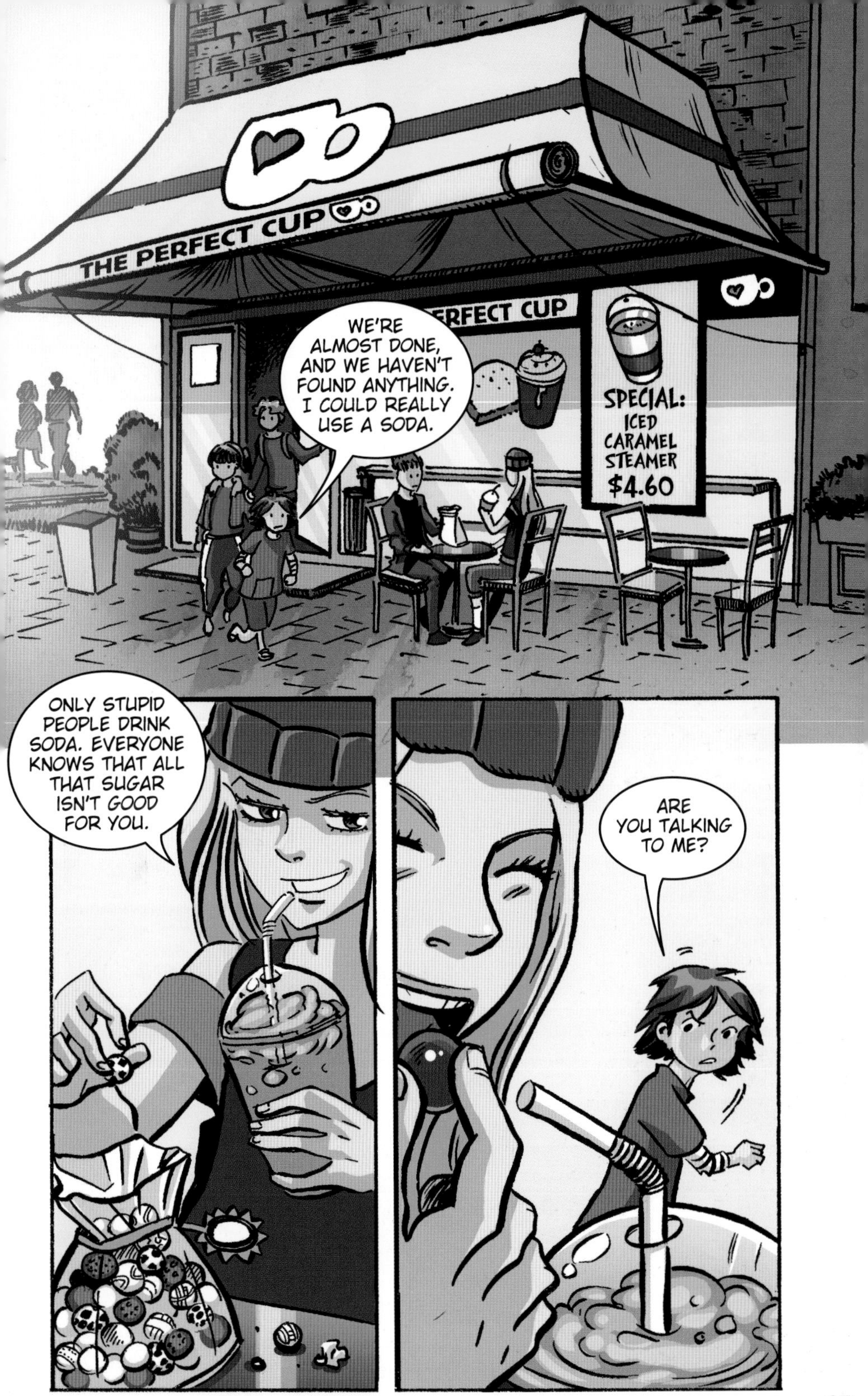
THE PERFECT CUP
SPECIAL: ICED CARAMEL STEAMER $4.60
WE'RE ALMOST DONE, AND WE HAVEN'T FOUND ANYTHING. I COULD REALLY USE A SODA.
ONLY STUPID PEOPLE DRINK SODA. EVERYONE KNOWS THAT ALL THAT SUGAR ISN'T GOOD FOR YOU.
ARE YOU TALKING TO ME?

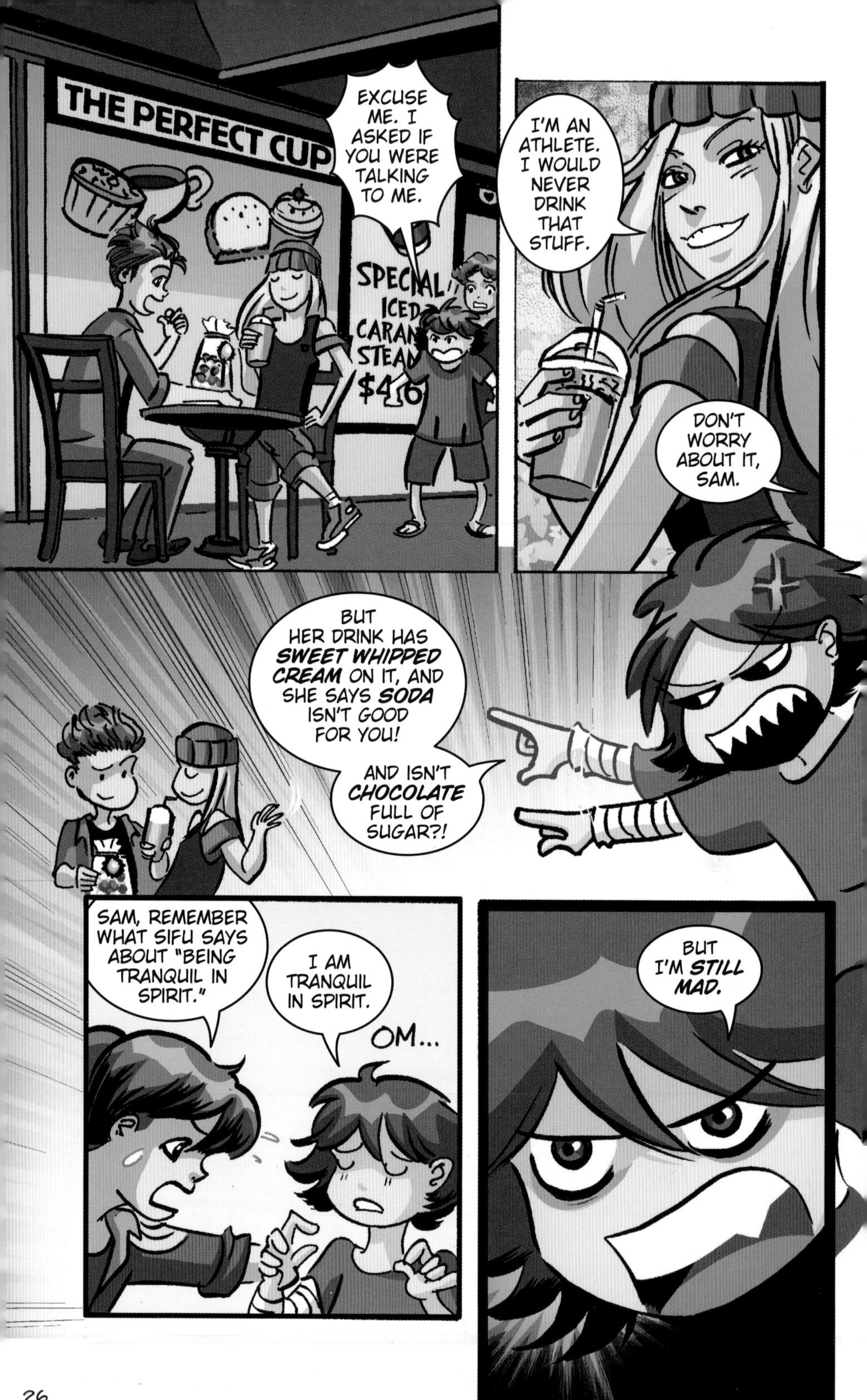
THE PERFECT CUP
EXCUSE ME. I ASKED IF YOU WERE TALKING TO ME.
SPECIAL ICED CARAM STEAM $4.6
I'M AN ATHLETE. I WOULD NEVER DRINK THAT STUFF.
DON'T WORRY ABOUT IT, SAM.
BUT HER DRINK HAS **SWEET WHIPPED CREAM** ON IT, AND SHE SAYS **SODA** ISN'T GOOD FOR YOU!
AND ISN'T **CHOCOLATE** FULL OF SUGAR?!
SAM, REMEMBER WHAT SIFU SAYS ABOUT "BEING TRANQUIL IN SPIRIT."
I AM TRANQUIL IN SPIRIT.
OM...
BUT I'M **STILL MAD.**

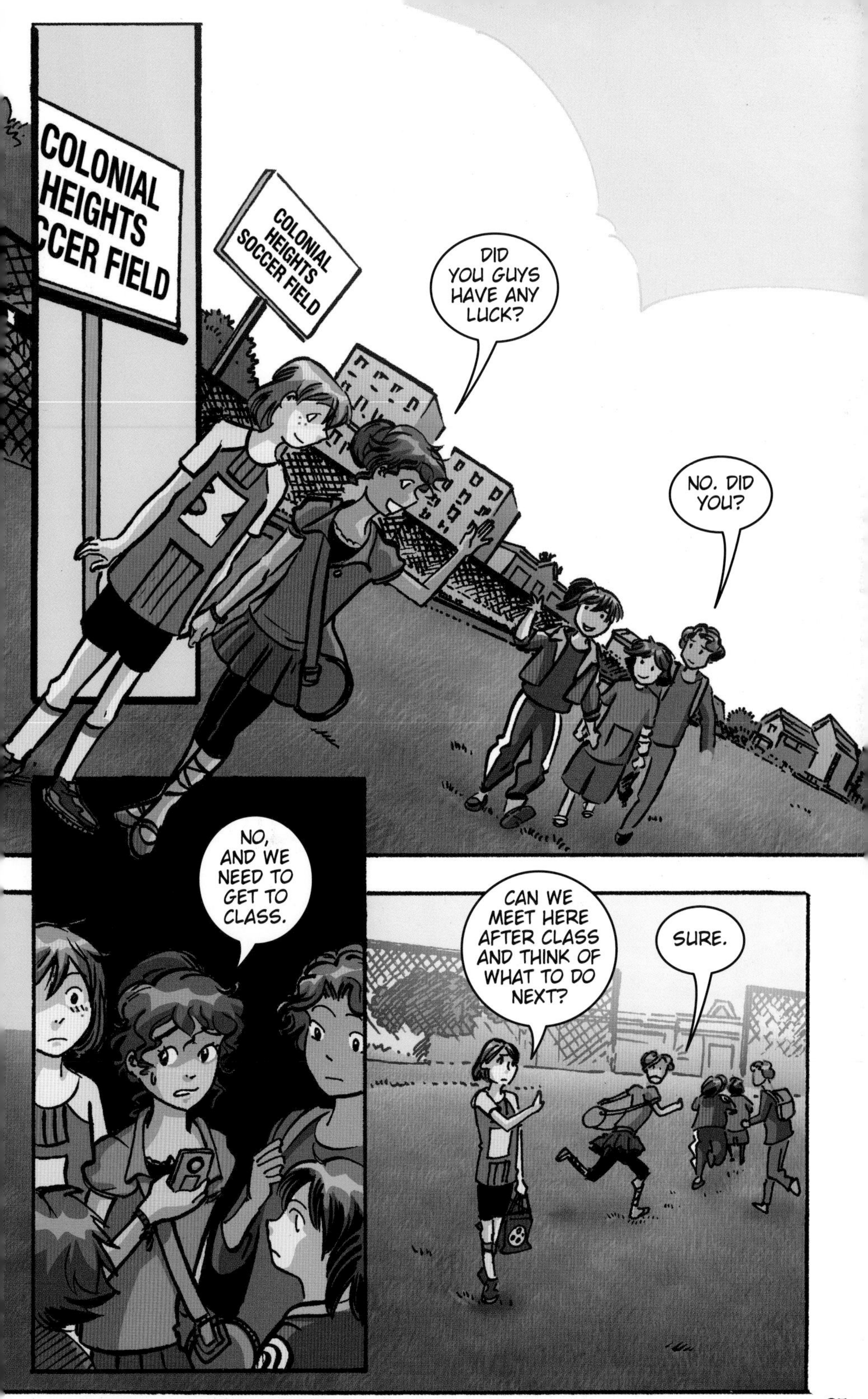
COLONIAL HEIGHTS CCER FIELD
COLONIAL HEIGHTS SOCCER FIELD
DID YOU GUYS HAVE ANY LUCK?
NO. DID YOU?
NO, AND WE NEED TO GET TO CLASS.
CAN WE MEET HERE AFTER CLASS AND THINK OF WHAT TO DO NEXT?
SURE.

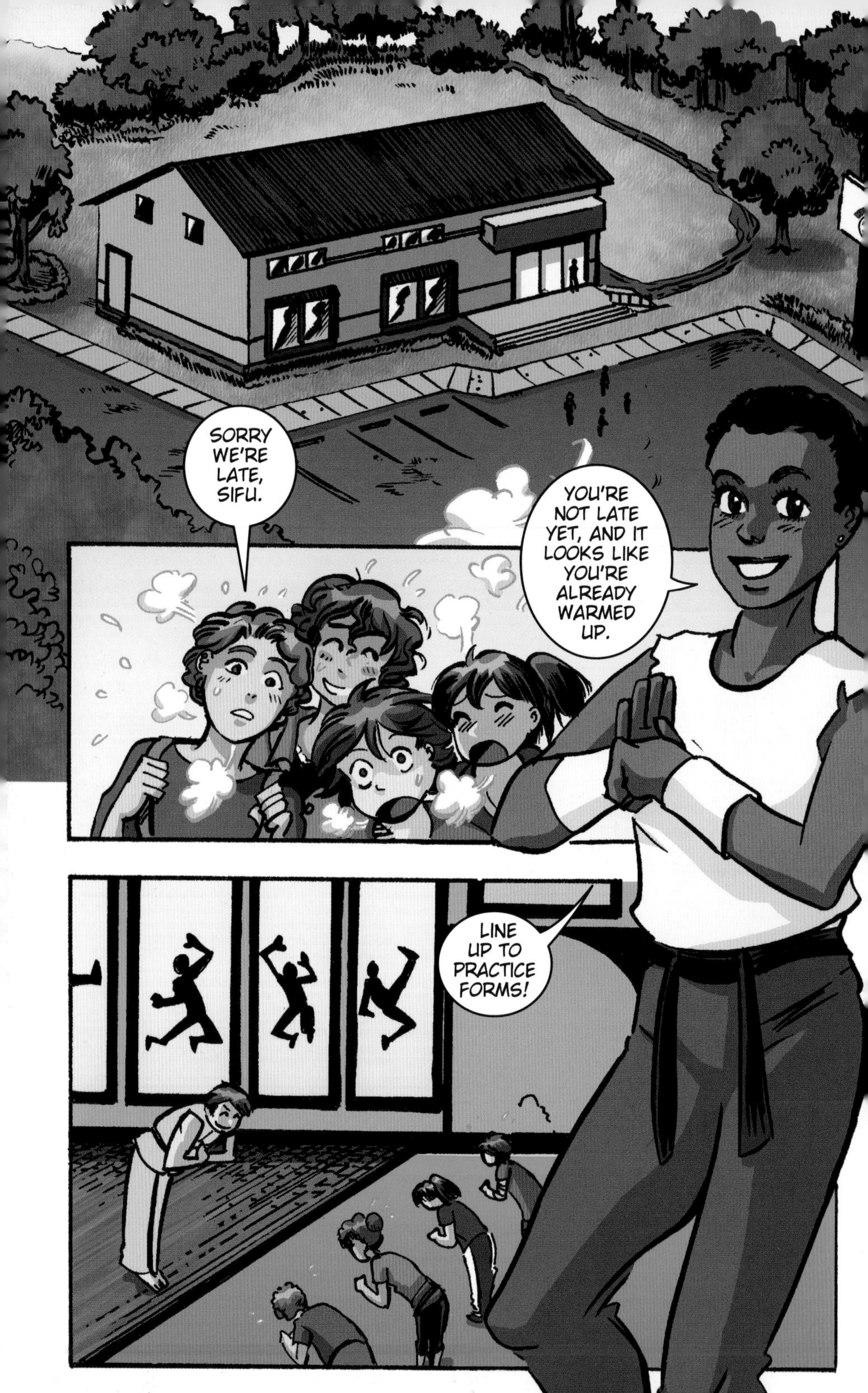

SORRY WE'RE LATE, SIFU.
YOU'RE NOT LATE YET, AND IT LOOKS LIKE YOU'RE ALREADY WARMED UP.
LINE UP TO PRACTICE FORMS!

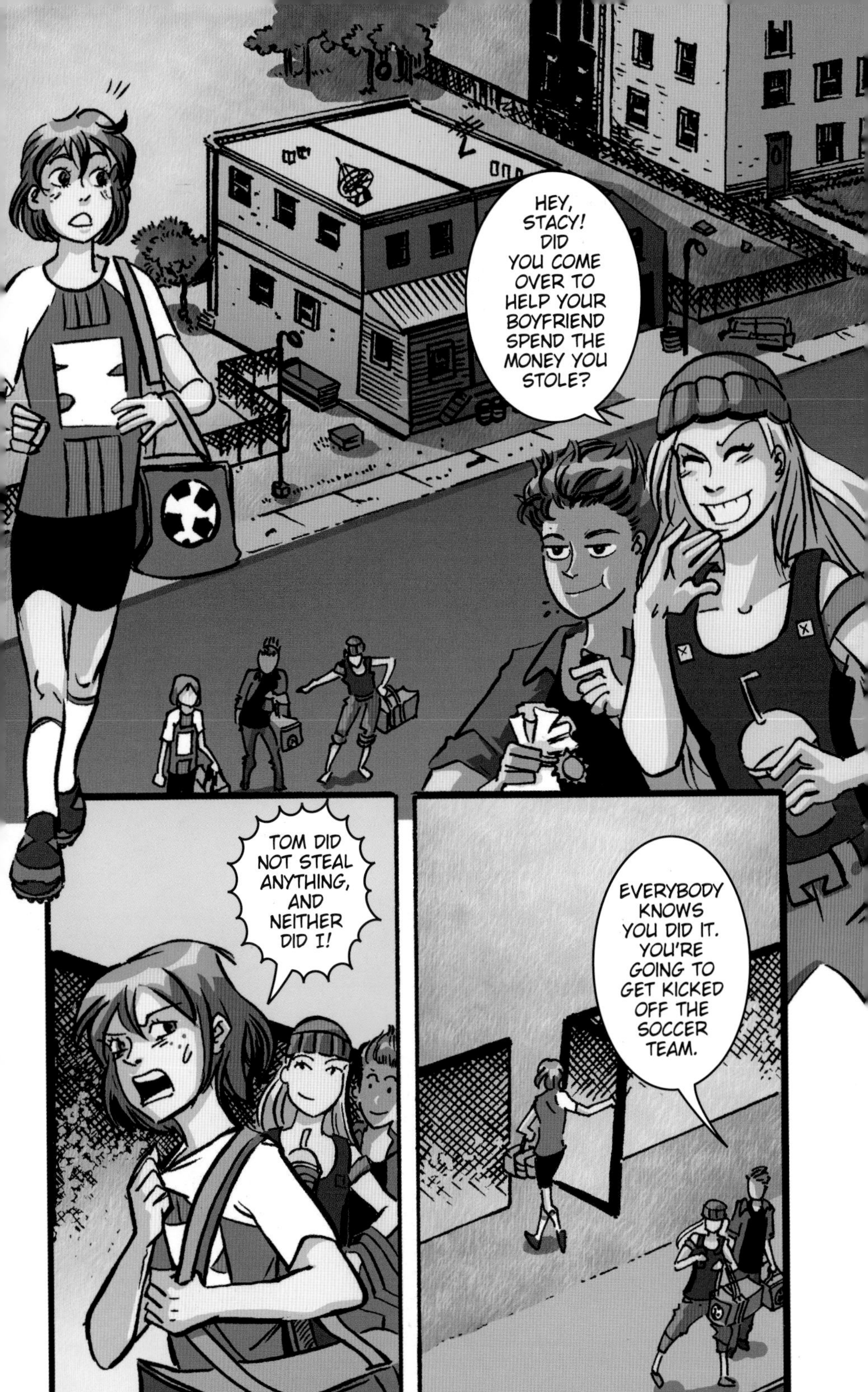
HEY, STACY! DID YOU COME OVER TO HELP YOUR BOYFRIEND SPEND THE MONEY YOU STOLE?
TOM DID NOT STEAL ANYTHING, AND NEITHER DID I!
EVERYBODY KNOWS YOU DID IT. YOU'RE GOING TO GET KICKED OFF THE SOCCER TEAM.

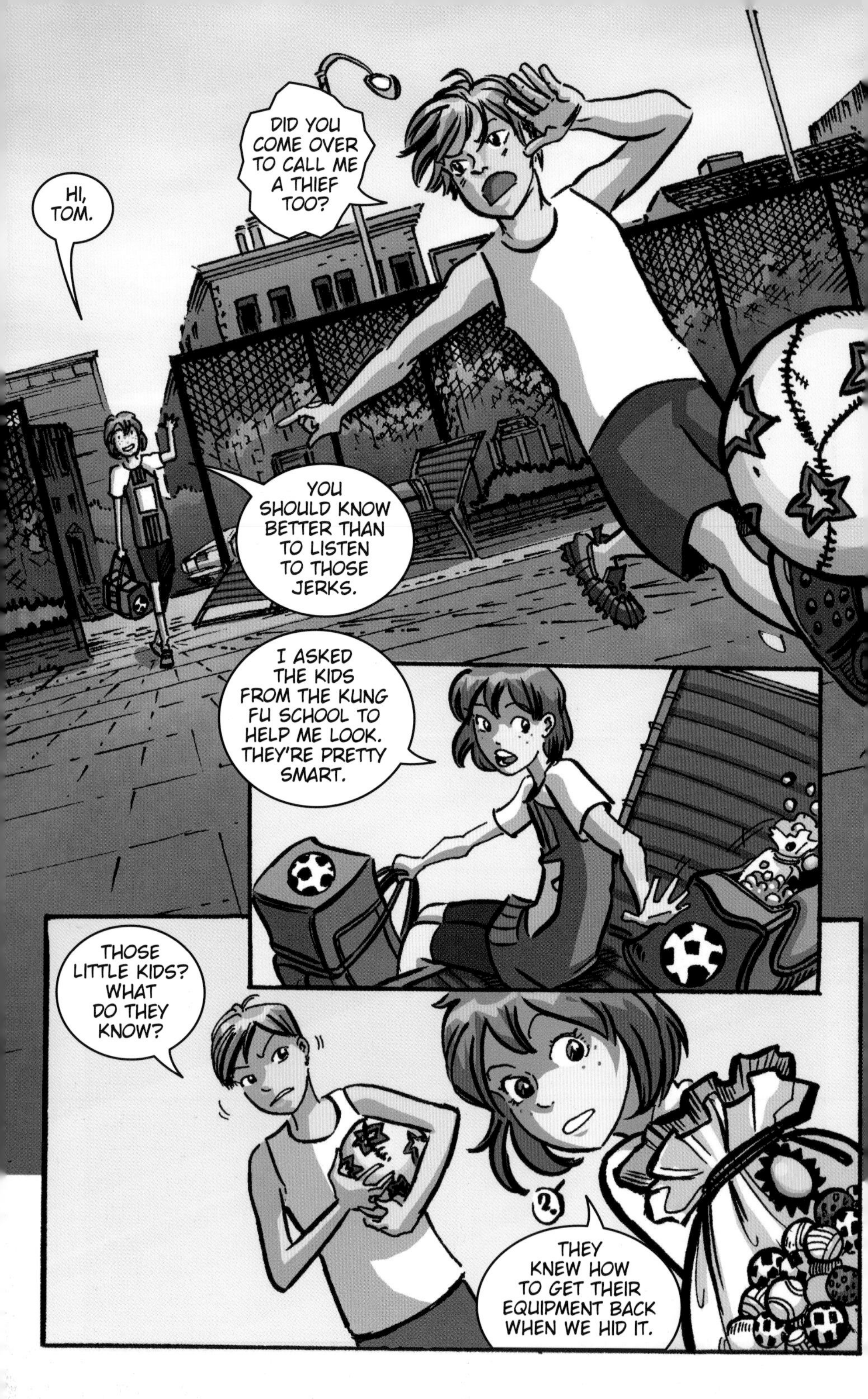
HI, TOM.
DID YOU COME OVER TO CALL ME A THIEF TOO?
YOU SHOULD KNOW BETTER THAN TO LISTEN TO THOSE JERKS.
I ASKED THE KIDS FROM THE KUNG FU SCHOOL TO HELP ME LOOK. THEY'RE PRETTY SMART.
THOSE LITTLE KIDS? WHAT DO THEY KNOW?
THEY KNEW HOW TO GET THEIR EQUIPMENT BACK WHEN WE HID IT.

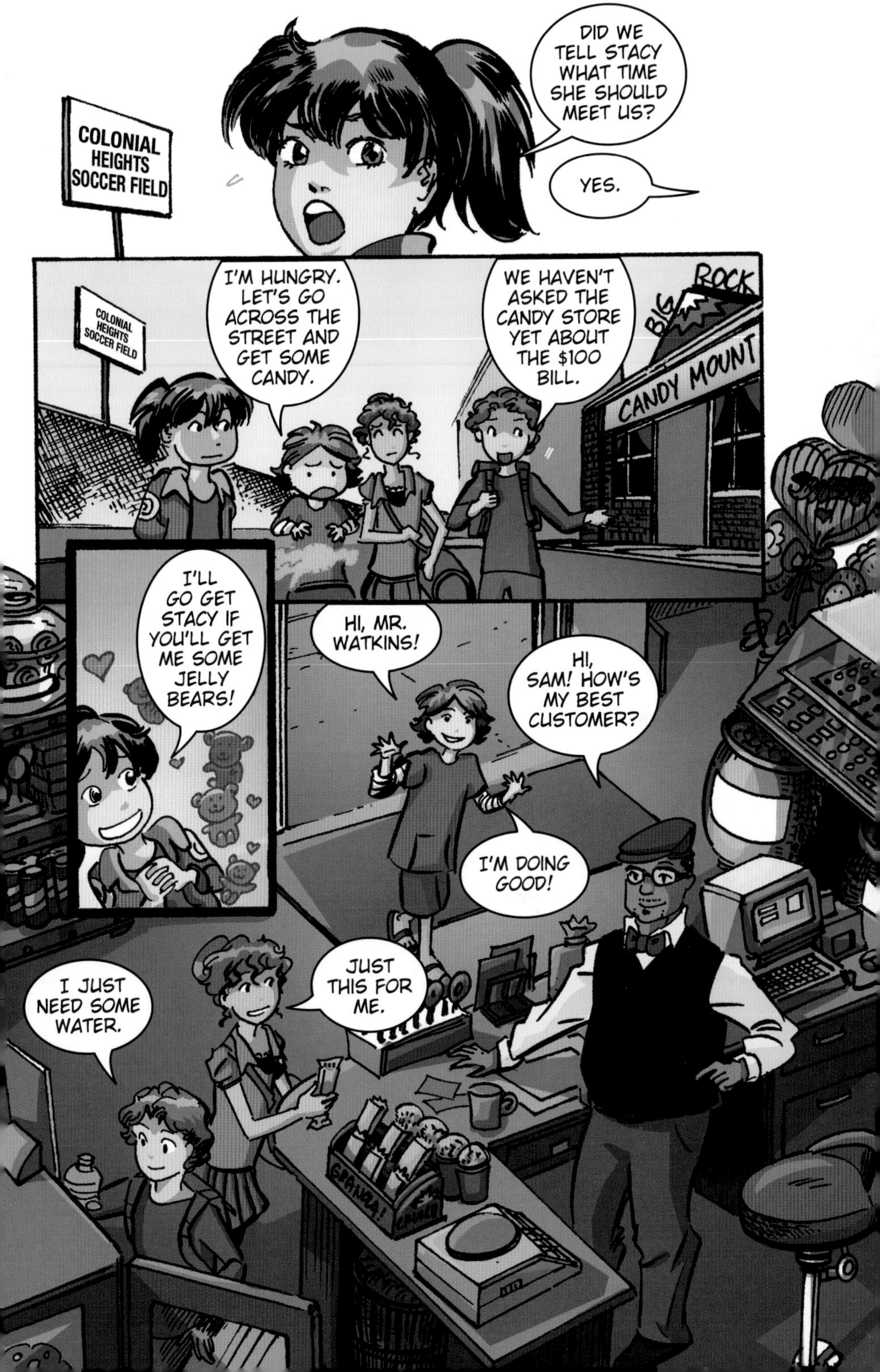
COLONIAL HEIGHTS SOCCER FIELD
DID WE TELL STACY WHAT TIME SHE SHOULD MEET US?
YES.
COLONIAL HEIGHTS SOCCER FIELD
I'M HUNGRY. LET'S GO ACROSS THE STREET AND GET SOME CANDY.
WE HAVEN'T ASKED THE CANDY STORE YET ABOUT THE $100 BILL.
BIG ROCK
CANDY MOUNT
I'LL GO GET STACY IF YOU'LL GET ME SOME JELLY BEARS!
HI, MR. WATKINS!
HI, SAM! HOW'S MY BEST CUSTOMER?
I'M DOING GOOD!
I JUST NEED SOME WATER.
JUST THIS FOR ME.

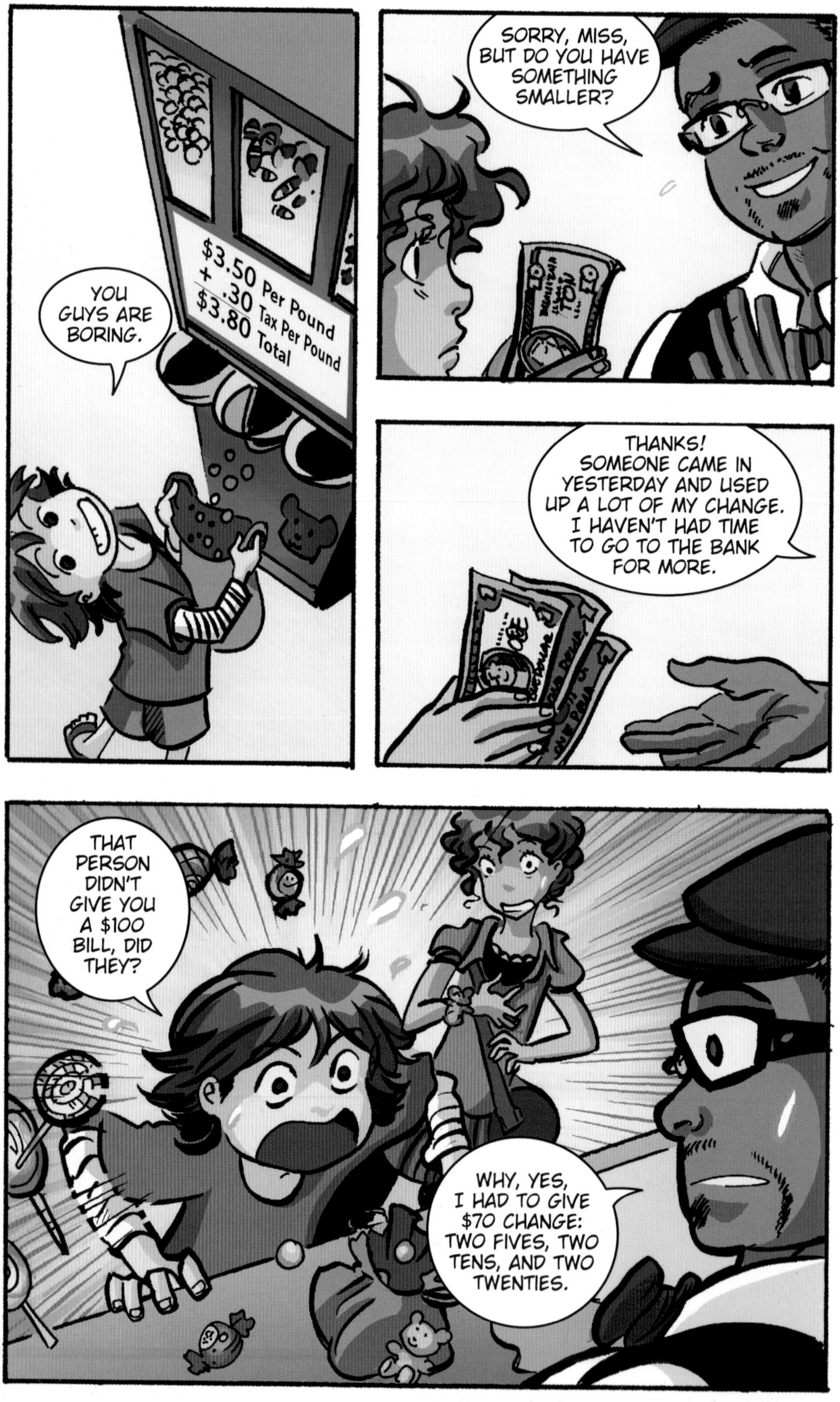

$3.50 Per Pound
+ .30 Tax Per Pound
$3.80 Total
YOU GUYS ARE BORING.
SORRY, MISS, BUT DO YOU HAVE SOMETHING SMALLER?
THANKS! SOMEONE CAME IN YESTERDAY AND USED UP A LOT OF MY CHANGE. I HAVEN'T HAD TIME TO GO TO THE BANK FOR MORE.
THAT PERSON DIDN'T GIVE YOU A $100 BILL, DID THEY?
WHY, YES, I HAD TO GIVE $70 CHANGE: TWO FIVES, TWO TENS, AND TWO TWENTIES.

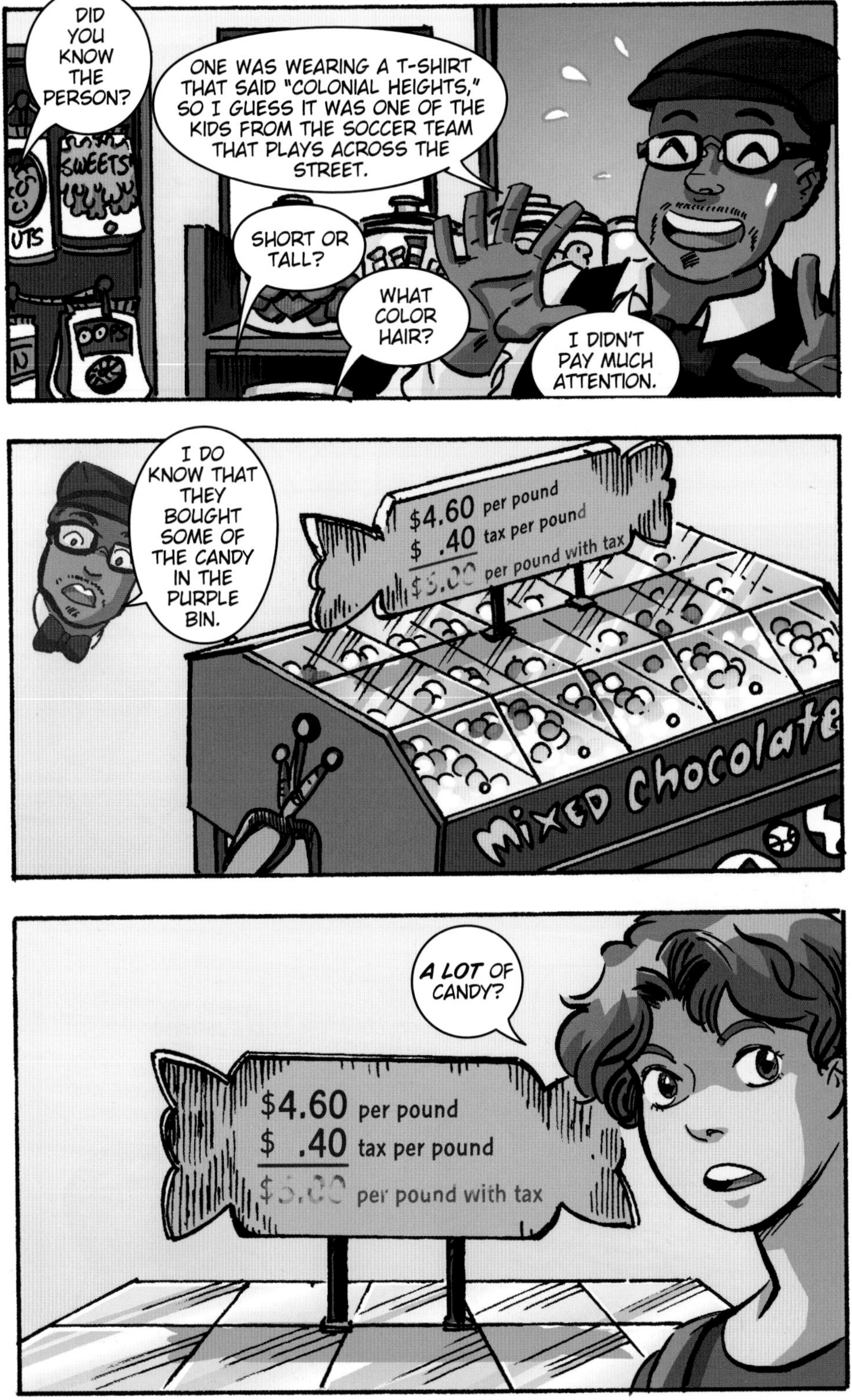
DID YOU KNOW THE PERSON?
ONE WAS WEARING A T-SHIRT THAT SAID "COLONIAL HEIGHTS," SO I GUESS IT WAS ONE OF THE KIDS FROM THE SOCCER TEAM THAT PLAYS ACROSS THE STREET.
SHORT OR TALL?
WHAT COLOR HAIR?
I DIDN'T PAY MUCH ATTENTION.
SWEETS
I DO KNOW THAT THEY BOUGHT SOME OF THE CANDY IN THE PURPLE BIN.
$4.60 per pound
$ .40 tax per pound
$5.00 per pound with tax
MIXED Chocolate
A LOT OF CANDY?
$4.60 per pound
$ .40 tax per pound
$5.00 per pound with tax

YOU CAN USE *DIVISION* TO FIND OUT HOW MUCH. IT COST $30, SO YOU DIVIDE $30 BY THE PRICE PER POUND.

BUT FIRST, WHY DO YOU NEED TO KNOW?

SOMEBODY STOLE A $100 BILL FROM A FRIEND OF OURS, AND WE THINK THEY SPENT IT HERE.

OH MY!

THE SIGN IS SMUDGED SO WE CAN'T READ HOW MUCH THE CANDY COST WITH TAX.

BUT WE KNOW THE PRICE IS $4.60, AND WE KNOW THE TAX IS $0.40. WE CAN ADD THEM TO FIND THE TOTAL.

$4.60 per pound
$ .40 tax per pound
$5.00 per pound with tax

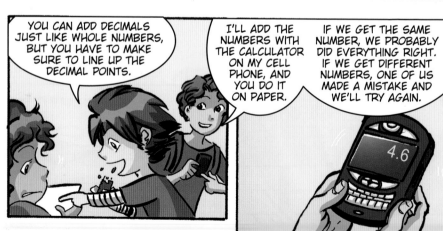

YOU CAN ADD DECIMALS JUST LIKE WHOLE NUMBERS, BUT YOU HAVE TO MAKE SURE TO LINE UP THE DECIMAL POINTS.

I'LL ADD THE NUMBERS WITH THE CALCULATOR ON MY CELL PHONE, AND YOU DO IT ON PAPER.

IF WE GET THE SAME NUMBER, WE PROBABLY DID EVERYTHING RIGHT. IF WE GET DIFFERENT NUMBERS, ONE OF US MADE A MISTAKE AND WE'LL TRY AGAIN.

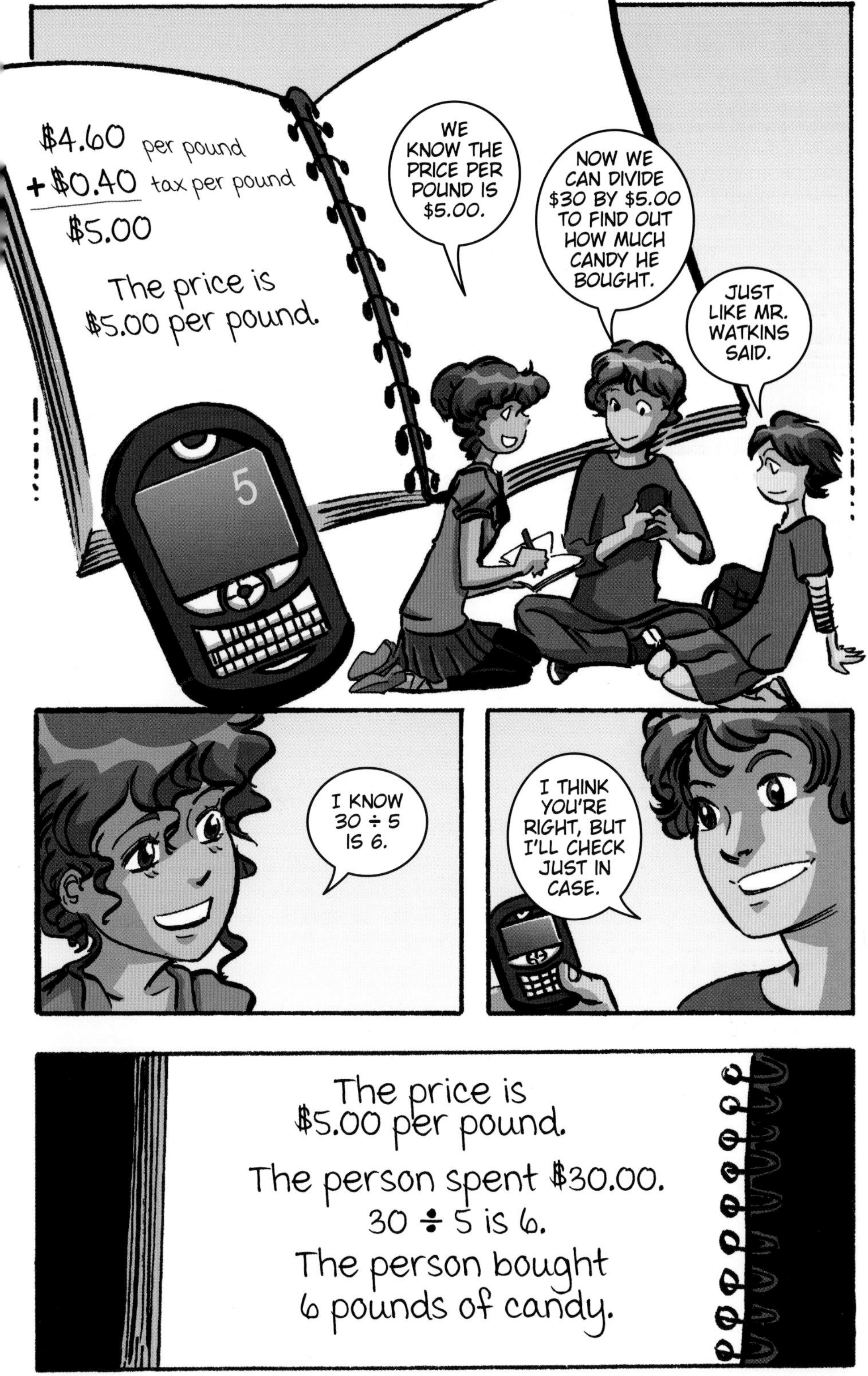
$4.60 per pound
+ $0.40 tax per pound
$5.00
The price is $5.00 per pound.
WE KNOW THE PRICE PER POUND IS $5.00.
NOW WE CAN DIVIDE $30 BY $5.00 TO FIND OUT HOW MUCH CANDY HE BOUGHT.
JUST LIKE MR. WATKINS SAID.
5
I KNOW 30 ÷ 5 IS 6.
I THINK YOU'RE RIGHT, BUT I'LL CHECK JUST IN CASE.
The price is $5.00 per pound.
The person spent $30.00.
30 ÷ 5 is 6.
The person bought 6 pounds of candy.

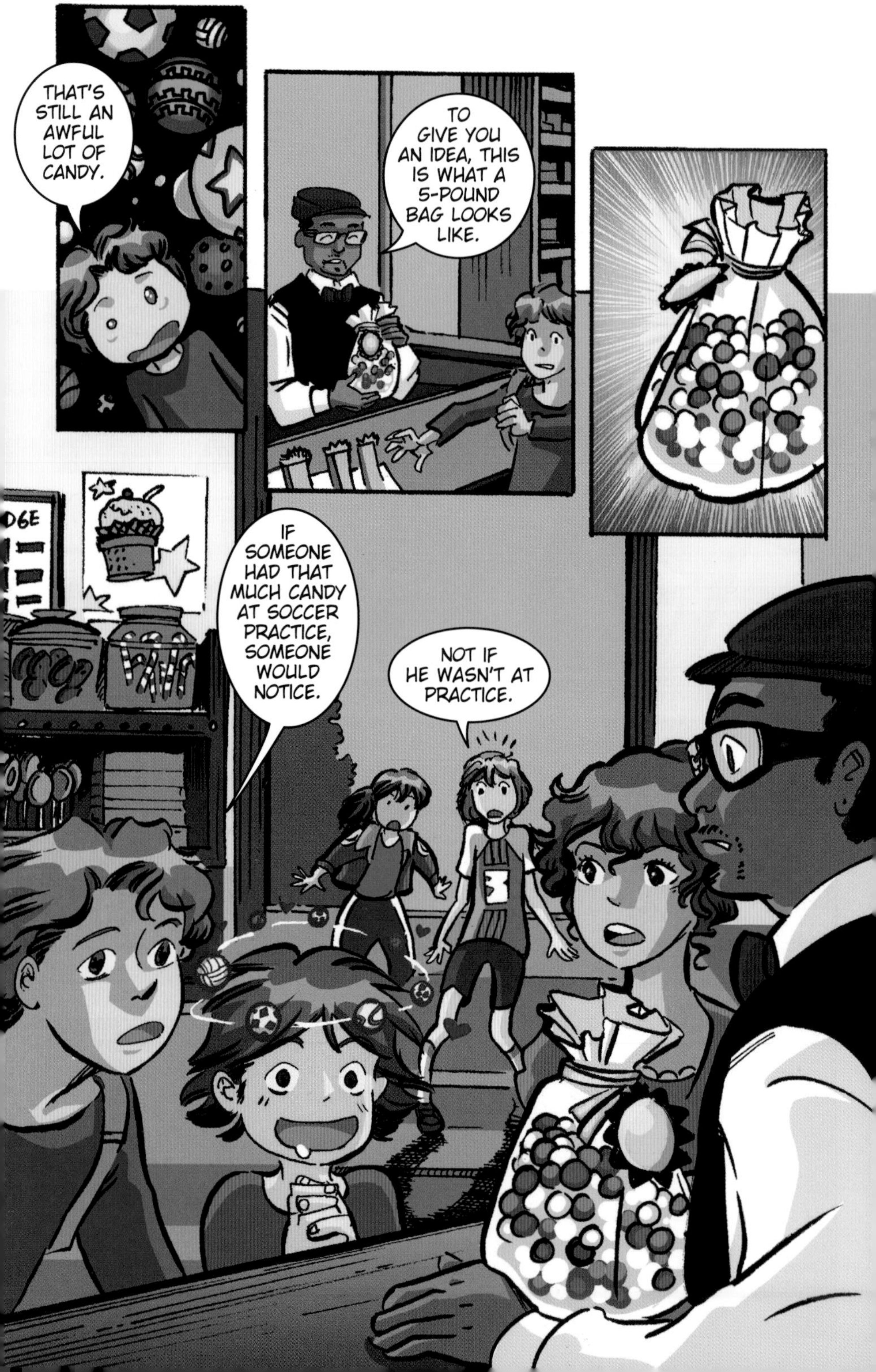
THAT'S STILL AN AWFUL LOT OF CANDY.
TO GIVE YOU AN IDEA, THIS IS WHAT A 5-POUND BAG LOOKS LIKE.
IF SOMEONE HAD THAT MUCH CANDY AT SOCCER PRACTICE, SOMEONE WOULD NOTICE.
NOT IF HE WASN'T AT PRACTICE.

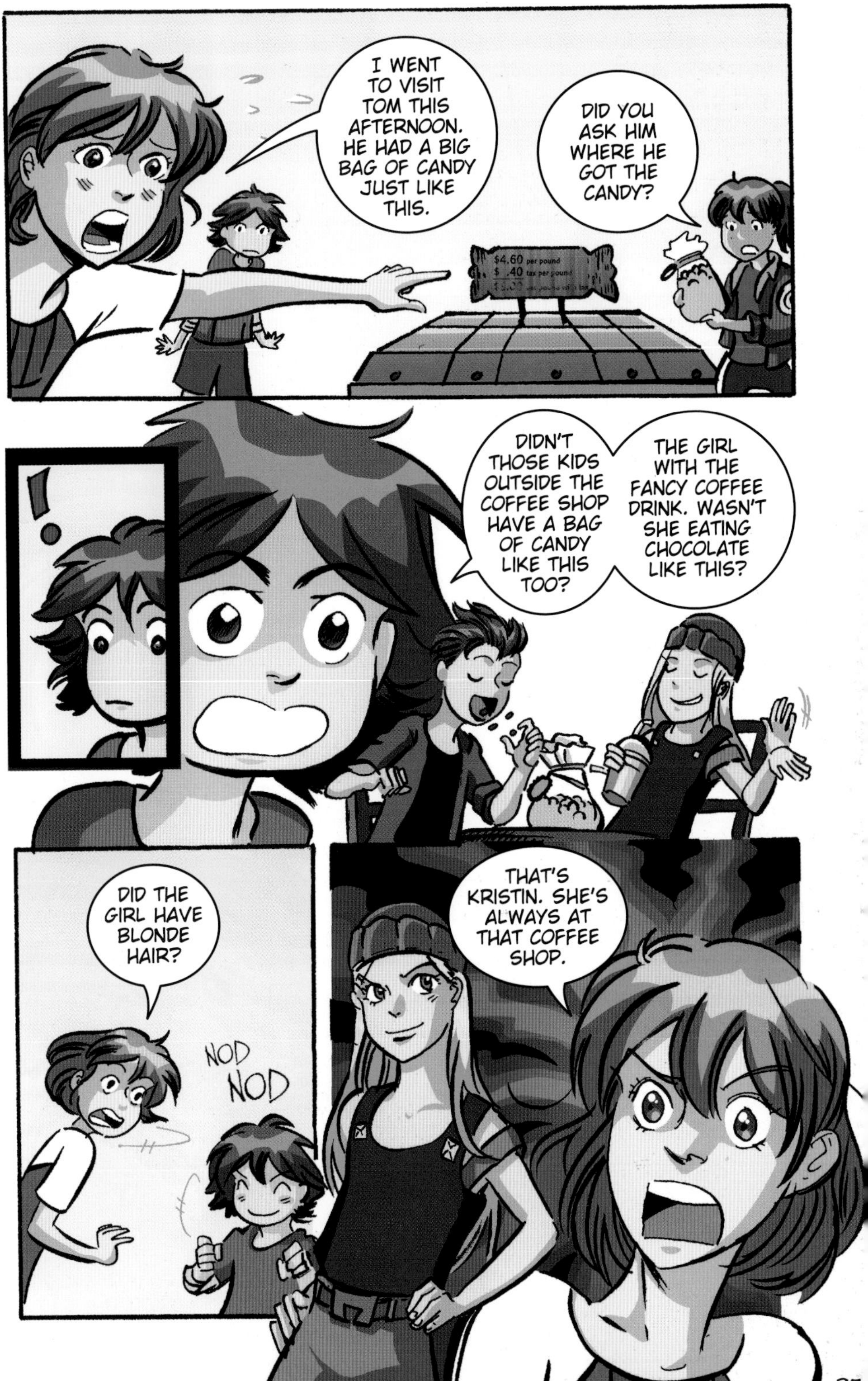

I WENT TO VISIT TOM THIS AFTERNOON. HE HAD A BIG BAG OF CANDY JUST LIKE THIS.
$4.60 per pound
$ .40 tax per pound
DID YOU ASK HIM WHERE HE GOT THE CANDY?
!
DIDN'T THOSE KIDS OUTSIDE THE COFFEE SHOP HAVE A BAG OF CANDY LIKE THIS TOO?
THE GIRL WITH THE FANCY COFFEE DRINK. WASN'T SHE EATING CHOCOLATE LIKE THIS?
DID THE GIRL HAVE BLONDE HAIR?
NOD
NOD
THAT'S KRISTIN. SHE'S ALWAYS AT THAT COFFEE SHOP.

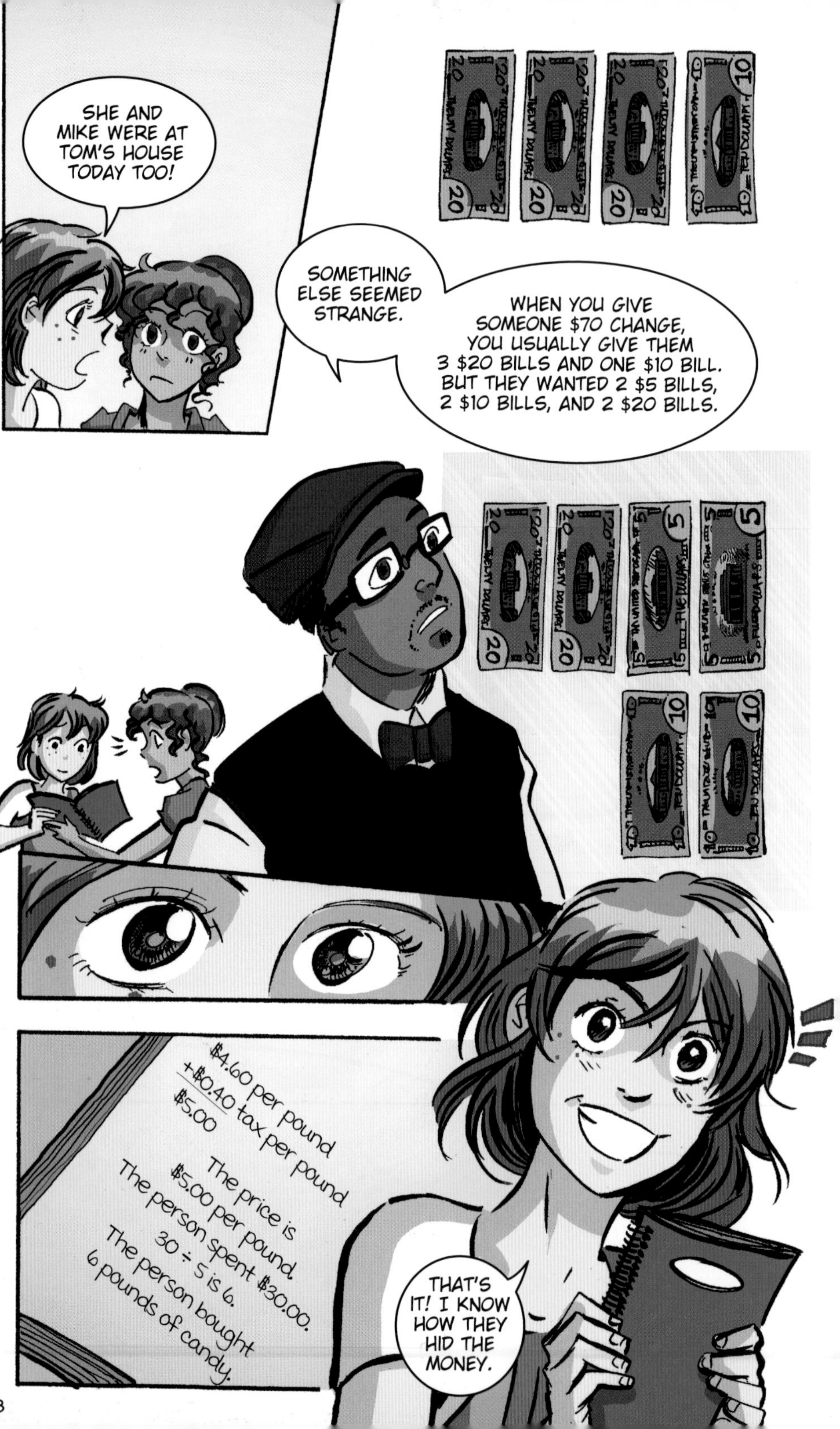
SHE AND MIKE WERE AT TOM'S HOUSE TODAY TOO!
SOMETHING ELSE SEEMED STRANGE.
WHEN YOU GIVE SOMEONE $70 CHANGE, YOU USUALLY GIVE THEM 3 $20 BILLS AND ONE $10 BILL. BUT THEY WANTED 2 $5 BILLS, 2 $10 BILLS, AND 2 $20 BILLS.
$4.60 per pound
+$0.40 tax per pound
$5.00
The price is $5.00 per pound.
The person spent $30.00.
30 ÷ 5 is 6.
The person bought 6 pounds of candy.
THAT'S IT! I KNOW HOW THEY HID THE MONEY.

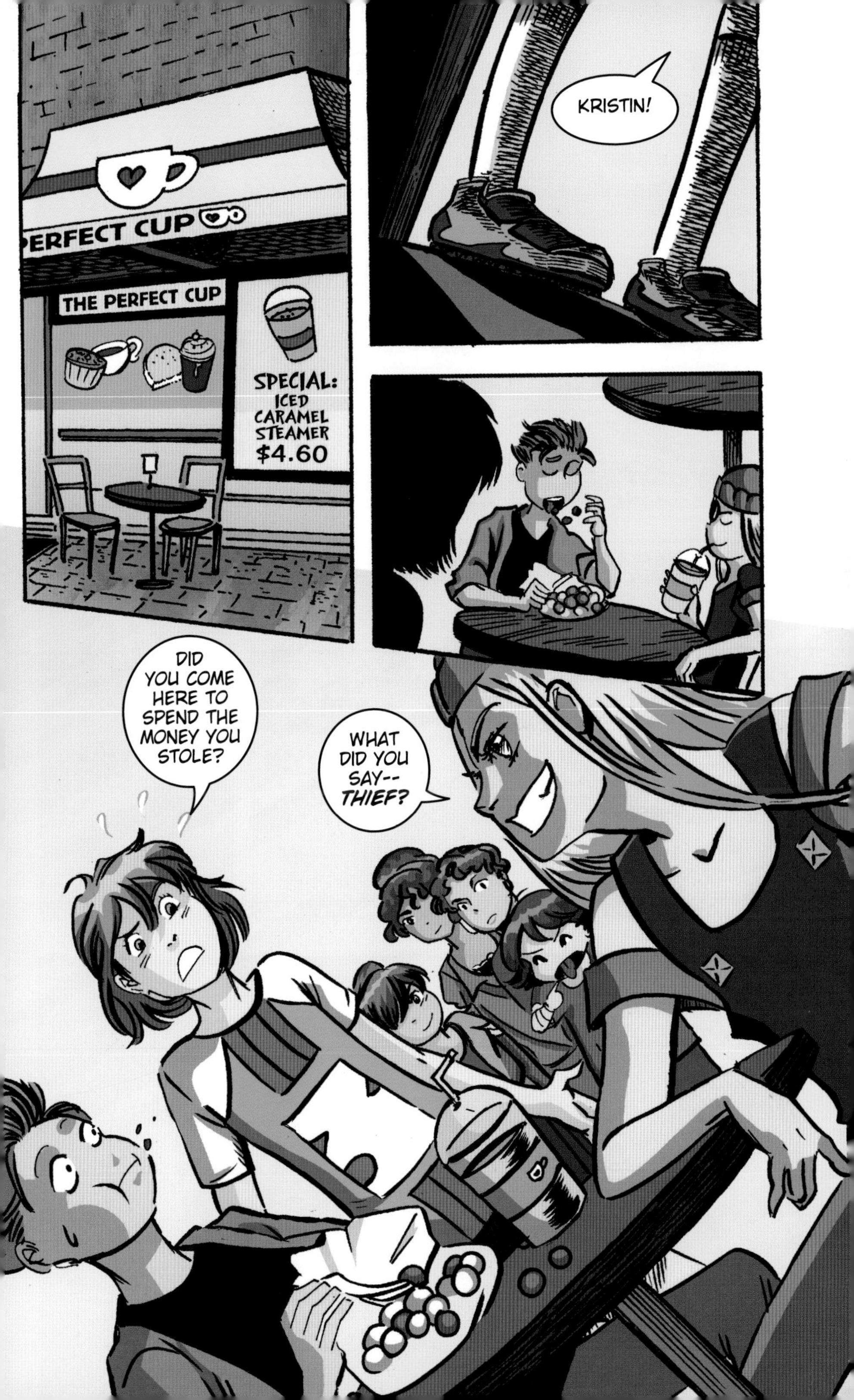
PERFECT CUP
THE PERFECT CUP
SPECIAL: ICED CARAMEL STEAMER $4.60
KRISTIN!
DID YOU COME HERE TO SPEND THE MONEY YOU STOLE?
WHAT DID YOU SAY-- *THIEF?*

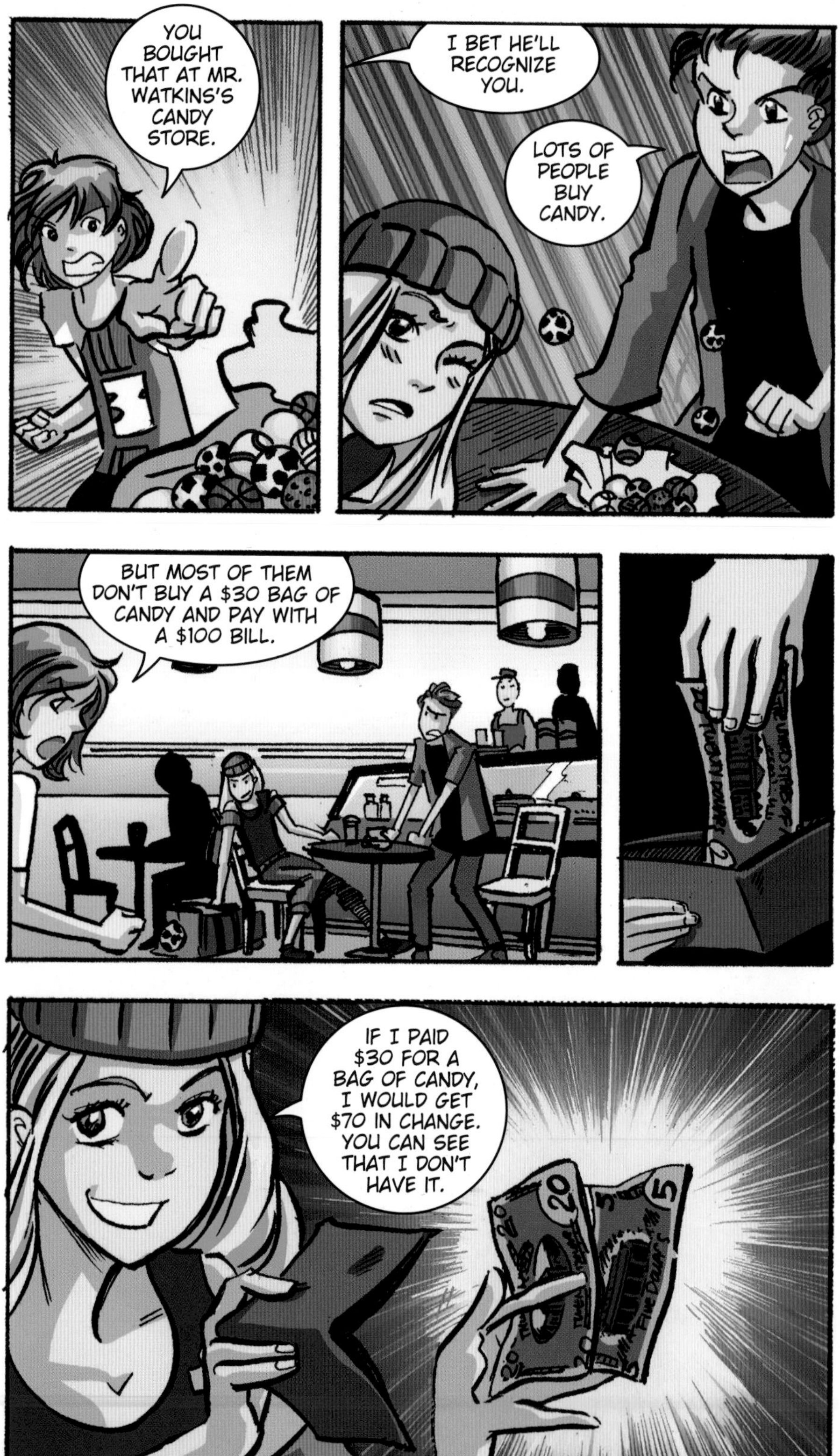
YOU BOUGHT THAT AT MR. WATKINS'S CANDY STORE.
I BET HE'LL RECOGNIZE YOU.
LOTS OF PEOPLE BUY CANDY.
BUT MOST OF THEM DON'T BUY A $30 BAG OF CANDY AND PAY WITH A $100 BILL.
IF I PAID $30 FOR A BAG OF CANDY, I WOULD GET $70 IN CHANGE. YOU CAN SEE THAT I DON'T HAVE IT.

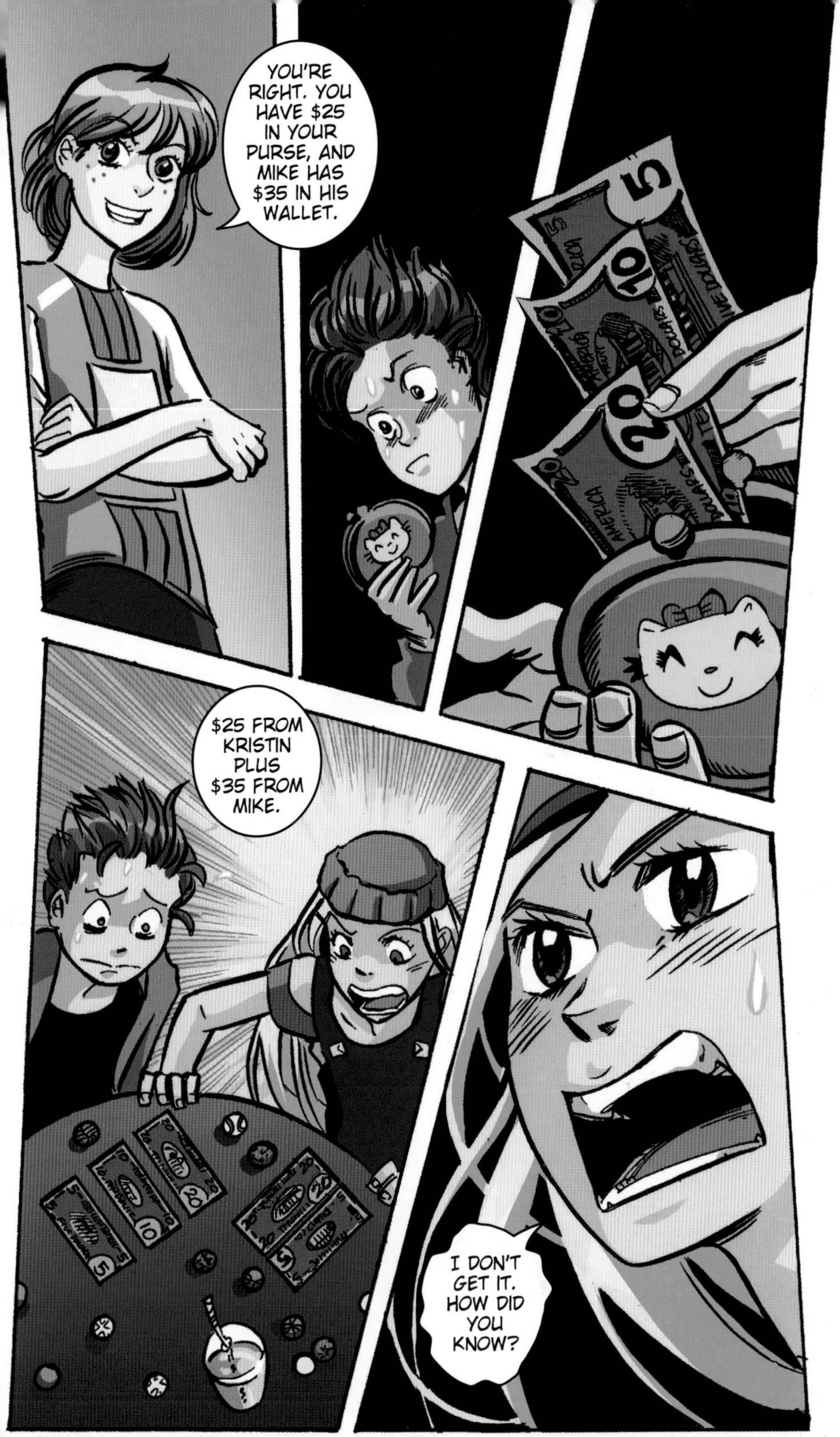
YOU'RE RIGHT. YOU HAVE $25 IN YOUR PURSE, AND MIKE HAS $35 IN HIS WALLET.
$25 FROM KRISTIN PLUS $35 FROM MIKE.
I DON'T GET IT. HOW DID YOU KNOW?

YOU TOOK THE $100 BILL OUT OF THE CASHBOX.

YOU WERE AFRAID SOMEONE WOULD SEE YOU WITH A $100 BILL, SO YOU BOUGHT SOMETHING.

YOU GOT MR. WATKINS TO GIVE YOU YOUR CHANGE IN A STRANGE WAY. YOU ASKED FOR 2 $20 BILLS, 2 $10 BILLS, AND 2 $5 BILLS.

THAT WAY YOU COULD EACH TAKE EXACTLY HALF OF THE REMAINING MONEY. THAT GAVE YOU $35 EACH.

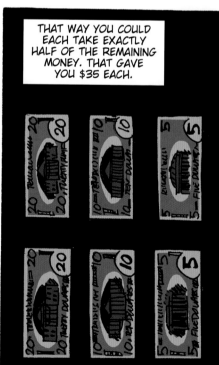

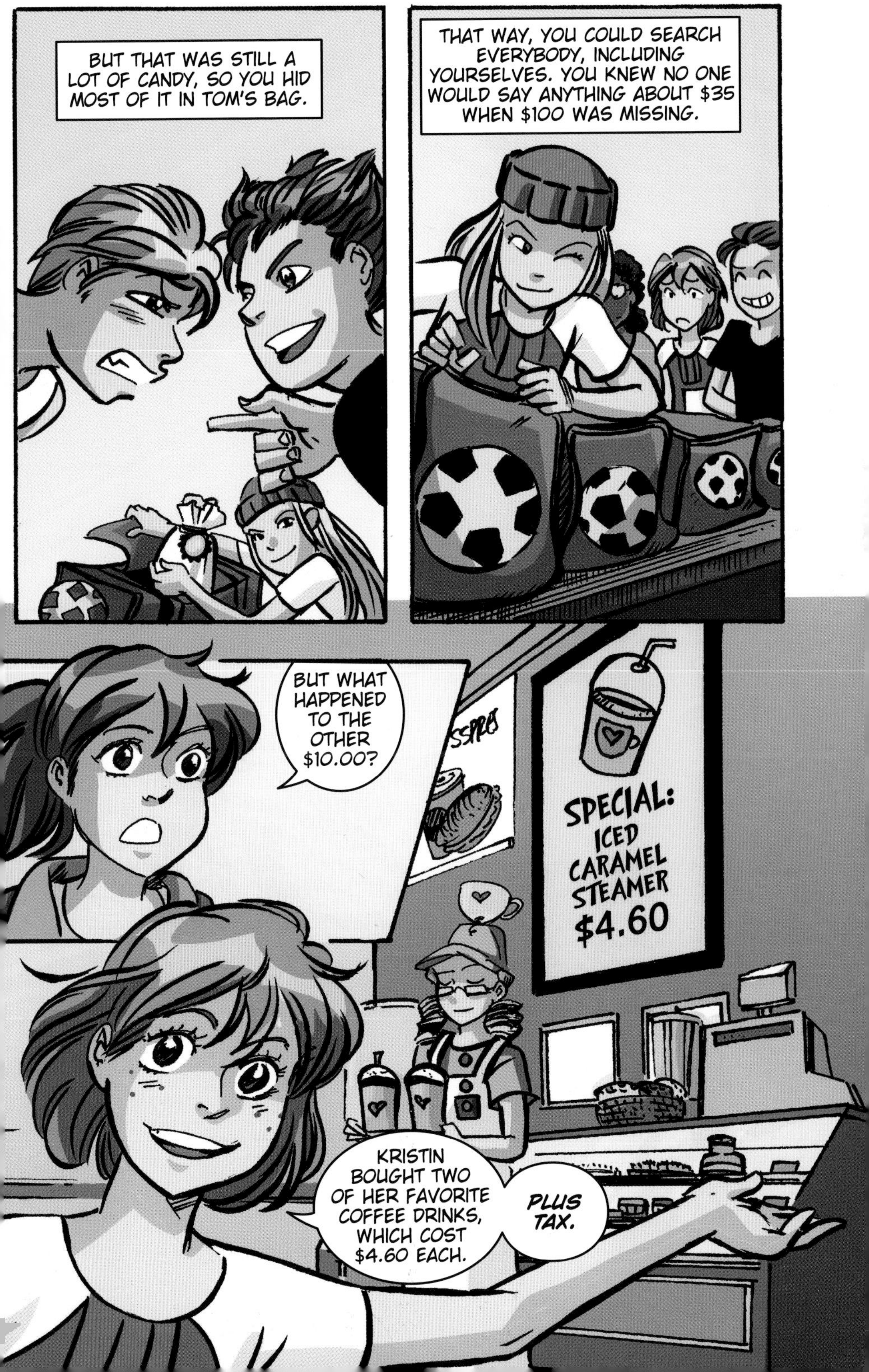
BUT THAT WAS STILL A LOT OF CANDY, SO YOU HID MOST OF IT IN TOM'S BAG.
THAT WAY, YOU COULD SEARCH EVERYBODY, INCLUDING YOURSELVES. YOU KNEW NO ONE WOULD SAY ANYTHING ABOUT $35 WHEN $100 WAS MISSING.
BUT WHAT HAPPENED TO THE OTHER $10.00?
SPECIAL: ICED CARAMEL STEAMER $4.60
KRISTIN BOUGHT TWO OF HER FAVORITE COFFEE DRINKS, WHICH COST $4.60 EACH.
PLUS TAX.

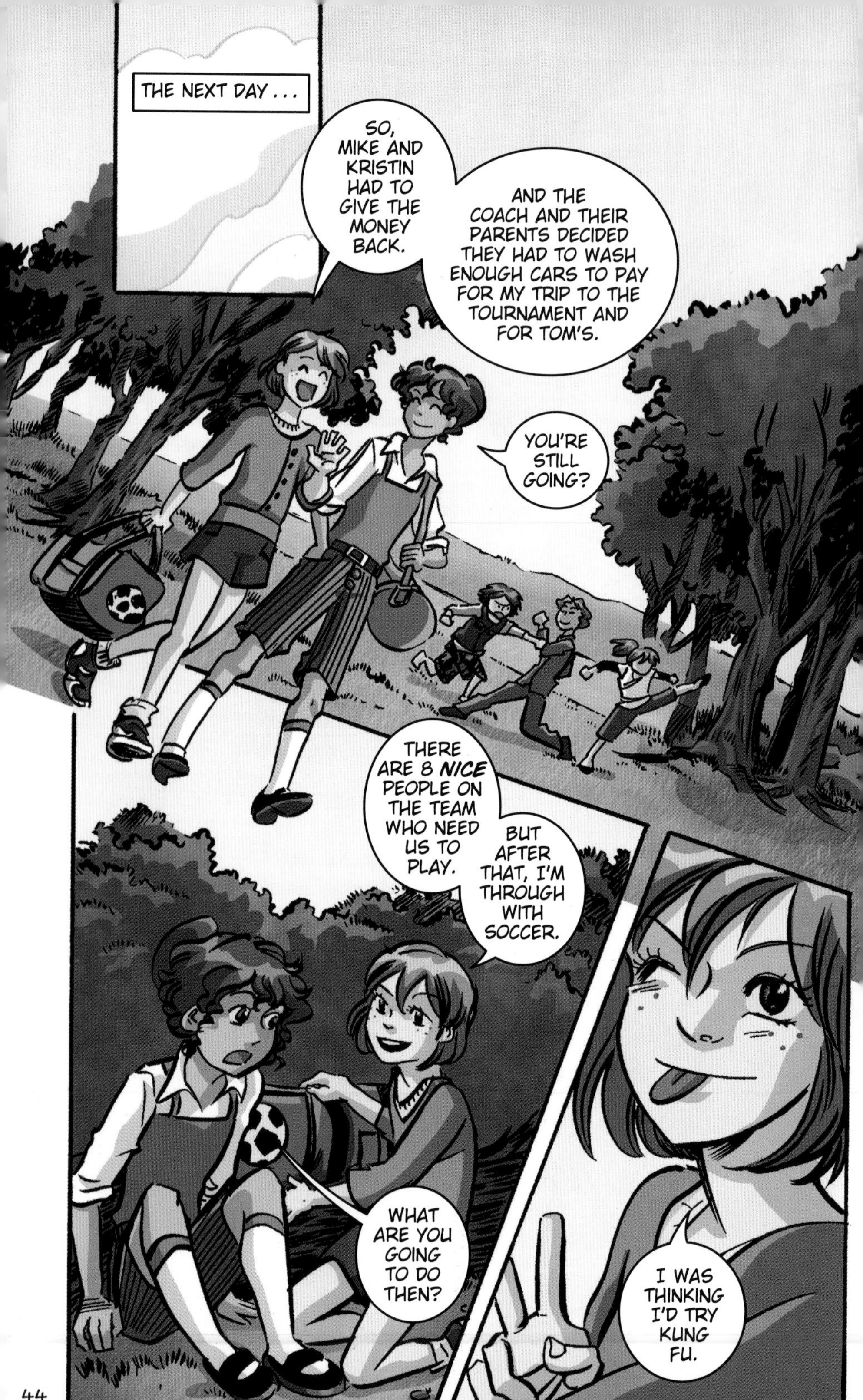
THE NEXT DAY . . .
SO, MIKE AND KRISTIN HAD TO GIVE THE MONEY BACK.
AND THE COACH AND THEIR PARENTS DECIDED THEY HAD TO WASH ENOUGH CARS TO PAY FOR MY TRIP TO THE TOURNAMENT AND FOR TOM'S.
YOU'RE STILL GOING?
THERE ARE 8 NICE PEOPLE ON THE TEAM WHO NEED US TO PLAY.
BUT AFTER THAT, I'M THROUGH WITH SOCCER.
WHAT ARE YOU GOING TO DO THEN?
I WAS THINKING I'D TRY KUNG FU.

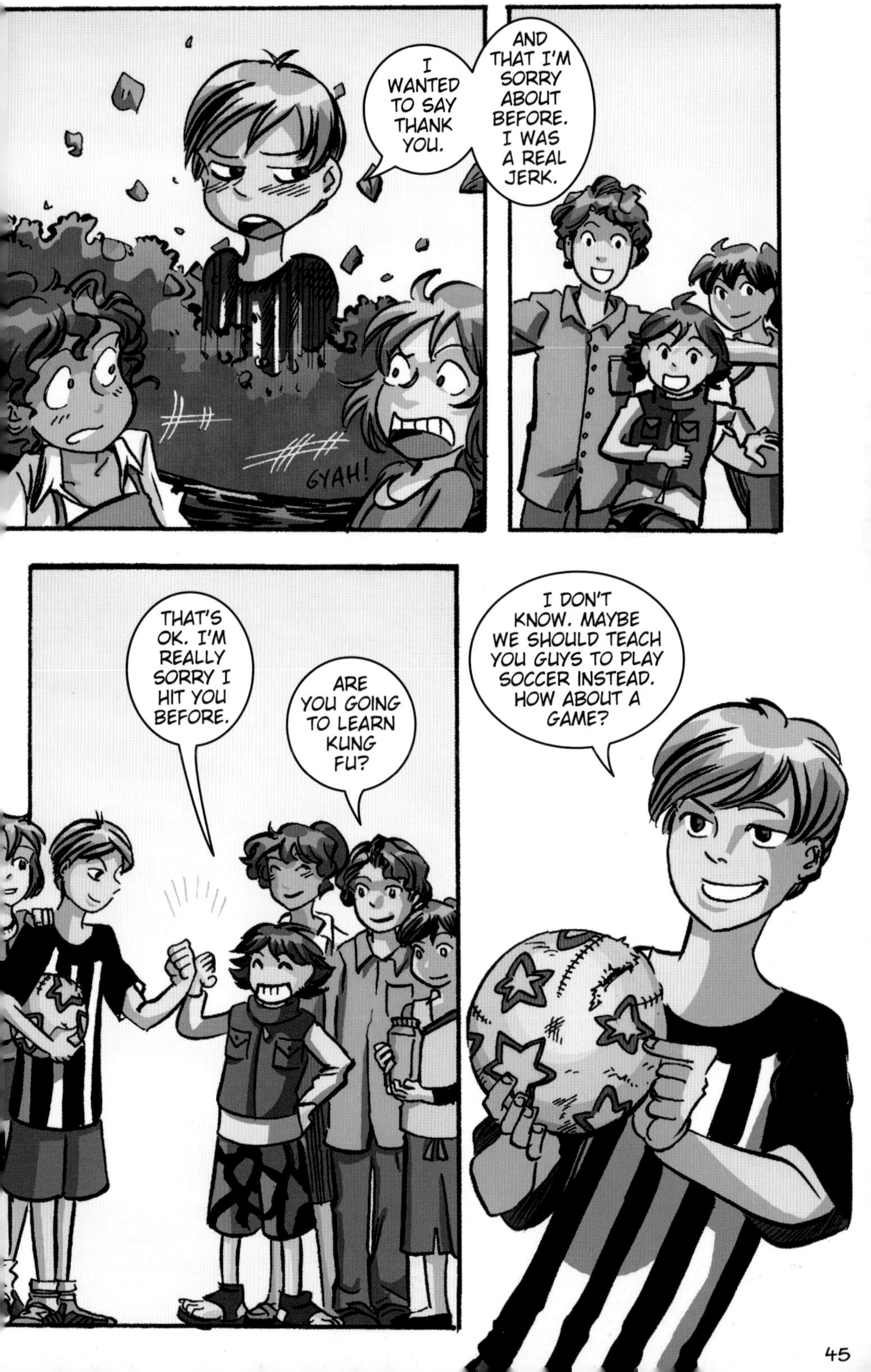

I WANTED TO SAY THANK YOU.
AND THAT I'M SORRY ABOUT BEFORE. I WAS A REAL JERK.
GYAH!
THAT'S OK. I'M REALLY SORRY I HIT YOU BEFORE.
ARE YOU GOING TO LEARN KUNG FU?
I DON'T KNOW. MAYBE WE SHOULD TEACH YOU GUYS TO PLAY SOCCER INSTEAD. HOW ABOUT A GAME?

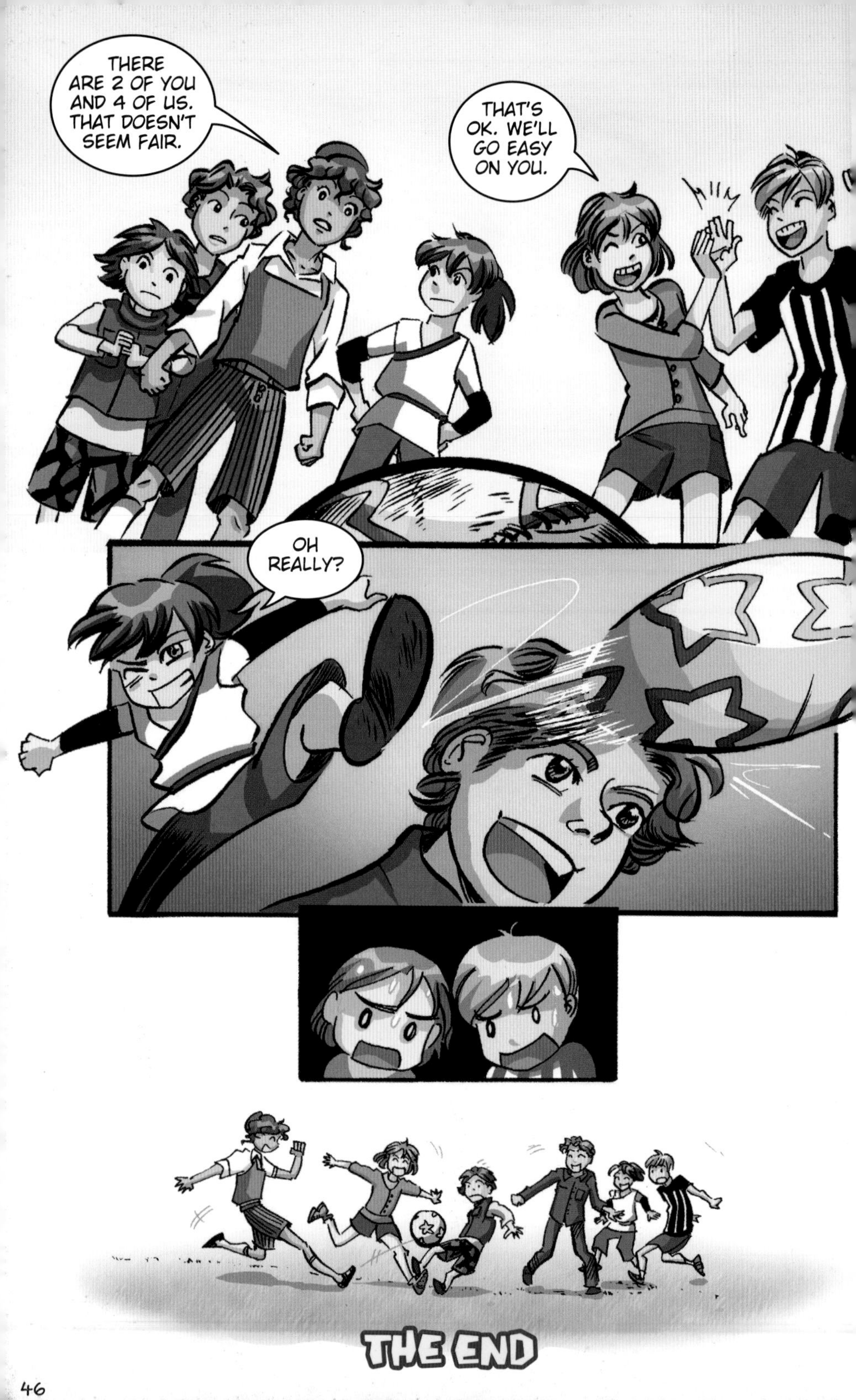
THERE ARE 2 OF YOU AND 4 OF US. THAT DOESN'T SEEM FAIR.
THAT'S OK. WE'LL GO EASY ON YOU.
OH REALLY?
THE END

The Author

Melinda Thielbar is a teacher who has written math courses for all ages, from kids to adults. In 2005 Melinda was awarded a VIGRE fellowship at North Carolina State University for PhD candidates "likely to make a strong contribution to education in mathematics." She lives in Raleigh, North Carolina, with her husband, author and video game programmer Richard Dansky, and their two cats.

The Artists

Tintin Pantoja was born in Manila in the Philippines. She received a degree in illustration and cartooning from the School of Visual Arts in New York City and was nominated for the Friends of Lulu "Best Newcomer" award. She was also a finalist in Tokyopop's Rising Stars of Manga 5. Her past books include a graphic novel version for kids of Shakespeare's play *Hamlet*.

Yuko Ota graduated from the Rochester Institute of Technology and lives in Maryland. She has worked as an animator and a lab assistant but is happiest drawing creatures and inventing worlds. She likes strong tea, the smell of new tires, and polydactyl cats (cats with extra toes!). She doesn't have any pets, but she has seven houseplants named Blue, Wolf, Charlene, Charlie, Roberto, Steven, and Doris.

Der-shing Helmer graduated with a degree in Biology from UC Berkeley, where she played with snakes and lizards all summer long. She is working toward becoming a biology teacher. When she is not tutoring kids, she likes to create art, especially comics. Her best friends are her two pet geckos (Smeg and Jerry), her king snake (Clarice), and the chinchilla that lives next door.

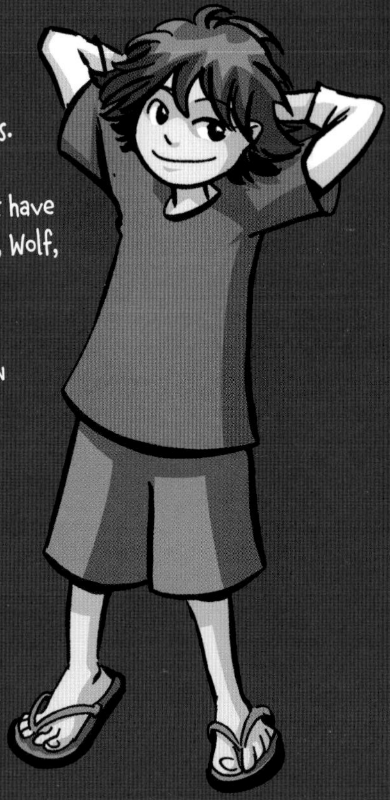

SAM BY TINTIN

START READING FROM THE OTHER SIDE OF THE BOOK!

This page would be the first page of a manga from Japan. This is because written Japanese is read from the right side of the page to the left side of the page. English is read from left to right, so this is the last page of this Manga Math Mystery. If you read the end of the book first, you'll spoil the mystery! Turn the book over so you can start on the first page. Then find the clues to the mystery with Sam, Joy, Amy, and Adam!

MANGA MATH MYSTERIES #3

Sam's little sister Michelle thinks there's a ghost in the creepy old house their dad bought. With help from a couple of friends on the soccer team, Sam, Amy, and Michelle use an old ghost story—plus measuring tools, distance, volume, and perimeters—to figure out the truth behind . . .

The Secret Ghost

MANGA MATH MYSTERIES

#1 THE LOST KEY A Mystery with Whole Numbers

#2 THE HUNDRED-DOLLAR ROBBER A Mystery with Money

#3 THE SECRET GHOST A Mystery with Distance and Measurement

#4 THE KUNG FU PUZZLE A Mystery with Time and Temperature